An Inexorable Mountie

Adventures of the First

Woman Mountie. Book 7

LAURIE SCHRAMM

Print ISBN: 978-1-7772424-4-2
ePub ISBN: 978-1-7772424-5-9

Laurie Schramm

Photo courtesy of VIA Rail Canada (Resource ID 1520).

Laurie Schramm

DEDICATION

To Cleo

Laurie Schramm

CONTENTS

Laurie Schramm

ACKNOWLEDGMENTS

I am extremely grateful to my supportive readers, especially Ann Marie, Katherine, William, and Jayme for their comments and suggestions on drafts of this book.

Special thanks also to three real-life veterans of the RCMP, all of whom have supplemented their encouragement with numerous background and factual reference materials on the Force: Chief Superintendent William Schramm (Ret.), who also kindly allowed my main character to borrow his Regimental Number, Assistant Commissioner Dawson Hovey (Ret.), and Staff Sergeant Al Lund (Ret., author of *Mounties on the Cover* and probably the world's leading authority on Mountie fiction).

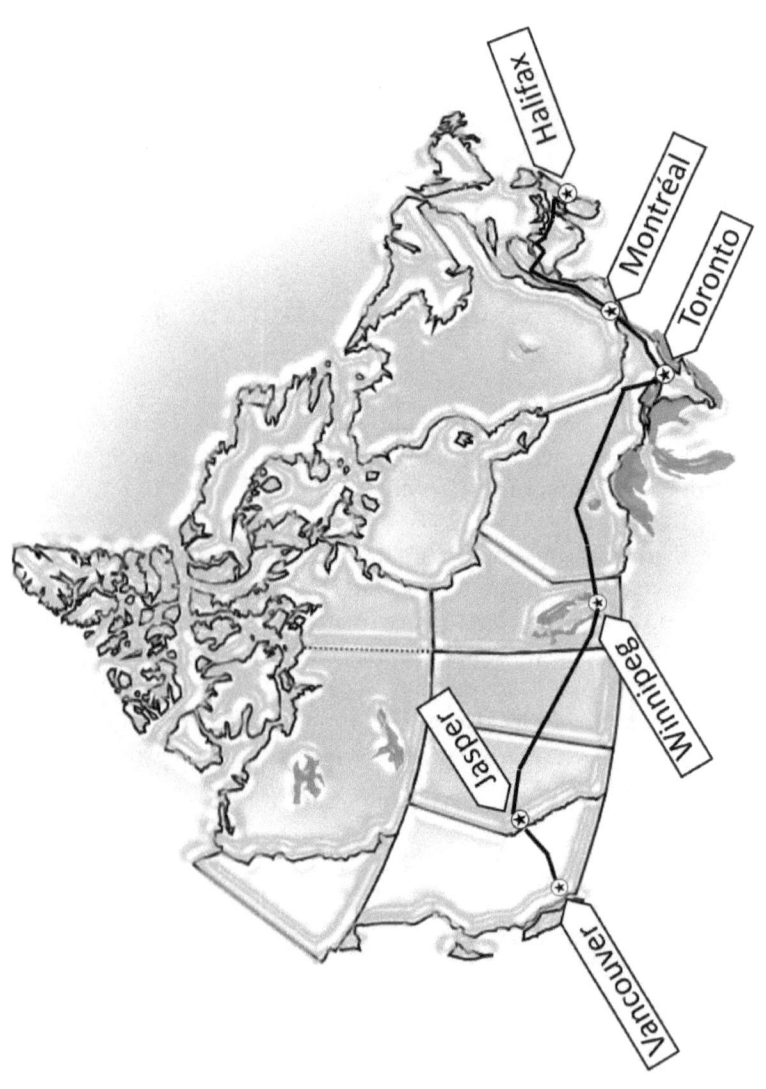

LIST OF CHARACTERS
(IN ORDER OF APPEARANCE)

- Jonathan (Jon) Hope, a thief
- Slim and Jess Peters, brother thieves
- Constable Alexandra (Alex) Houston, RCMP
- Silver, an Alaskan Malamute. Alex's friend and companion
- Constable Jack McDonald, RCMP
- Assistant Commissioner George MacLeod, RCMP
- Staff Sergeant Robert (Bob) G. Simpson, RCMP
- Oliver Risk, American Businessman
- Jonathan (Nathan) Risk, United Church Minister
- François Boucher, VIA Rail Conductor
- Colonel James Peters, retired Canadian Army Veteran
- Hannah Peters, daughter of Colonel Peters
- Benjamin (Ben) Shaw, a bit of a mystery
- Cleo, an orange, black, and white Calico Cat
- Émile Cournoyer, VIA Rail Attendant

Laurie Schramm

1 PRELUDE: A ROBBERY

August 2, 1920
Canada's Rocky Mountains,
Somewhere on the British Columbia side

"Are you ready Jon?"

Jonathon (Jon) Hope was a young man of average height and slender build. He was unremarkable, in fact, except possibly for his youth and his bright, clear eyes. He didn't look like a con-man, cheater, or thief but he was, unquestionably, all three.

"Yes, I think it's time," he replied. "Are you ready to ride?" he asked his two companions, Slim and Jess Peters, who were busily tying their axes to the saddles on their horses. When they were finished, all three men mounted up.

"Ready boss. Let's go," replied Jess. Jess and Slim were brothers. Jess was the talkative one, while Slim, for his part, simply nodded.

It was a small gang. If, that is, a group of three men could be called a gang. Whereas a discerning observer might have found fault with the men's rough appearances, it would have been difficult indeed to find fault with their horses. These latter were uniformly fine specimens of their species. Young, healthy, and strong looking, these were horses that had been well cared for. They could be counted on to maintain sure footing, speed, and endurance — all qualities that would shortly be needed.

The three men rode into the nearby forest and disappeared into the first

1

game trail they encountered.

***

Train number 63[1] of the Canadian Pacific Railroad had just exited from one of the many tunnels and snow sheds that protected its journey through the Rocky Mountains, and was now in an open clearing. It would have made a fine sight, comprising as it did one of the grand steam locomotives of the pre-diesel era, its tender (to provide its fuel and water), two passenger cars, a baggage car, an express car, and the ubiquitous red caboose (or crew car). Now that it was clear of the latest tunnel, the train slowly gained speed as it purposefully rolled along its track, in parallel with a rocky stream that was flush with meltwater from the glaciers and snowfields that lie high above. As the train began to gain altitude, the engineer looked ahead to the next patch of forest, swore loudly, and opened the steam valve to throttle back the engine.

Up ahead, at the entrance to the forest, a large tree had fallen and was lying diagonally across the tracks. As the train began to slow, the engineer began applying the steam brake. The fireman, who had by now seen the fallen tree, pulled the whistle cord with sharp tugs so that the locomotive's throaty steam whistle would produce a succession of short blasts. This was their standard method of alerting the conductor, and the two trainmen at the back of the train, that something — usually people or livestock - was on the track. In this case it also served as a warning to two armed guards in the express car that there might be more to this obstruction than met the eye.

There was only the one tree lying on the rails, and the pointed shape of the end combined with the similarly pointed shape of the stump suggested that it had been felled by beavers. The trainmen had seen things like this before and were prepared. Within a matter of minutes, one end of a heavy chain had been attached to the bottom of the tree, with the other end being attached to a standing tree of the forest fringe that was several yards away from the tracks. One end of another heavy chain was then attached to the top of the fallen tree, with the other end attached to the 'cow-catcher' at the front of the locomotive, which had been inched forward for this purpose. Then, with the train in reverse, the second chain straightened out and pulled the tree more or less parallel to the tracks. As the train continued to reverse, the first chain straightened out, which pulled the bottom of the tree away from the tracks. When this was done, the tree lay diagonally away from, and sufficiently clear of the tracks. After that, it was simply a matter of untying the chains, stowing them away, and re-boarding the train.

As the engineer shifted the locomotive back to forward gear and opened the throttle, the train slowly resumed its entrance into the forest and the crew began to relax.

That was a mistake.

Whether the train's crew was tired, inattentive, or both will never be known.

Perhaps it was simply the nearness of the forest that now bordered the train's right of way — providing a false sense of security.

Perhaps the shadows cast by the tall trees prevented anyone from seeing what came next.

Crouched low, Jess darted out of the forest and climbed up the steps at the rear of the locomotive. By the time the train's engineer and fireman turned and realized they had company, Jess was pointing two double-action U.S. Army Colt .45 revolvers[2] at them. To the crew they simply looked big, dark, and menacing.

"Keep your hands where I can see them, please," said Jess, "and stop the train – NOW!"

Although spoken politely, there was no mistaking his seriousness.

At this point, only the locomotive and the first few cars were actually in the forest. The rest of the cars were still in the clearing.

When the engineer had complied and the train came to a full stop, Jess told them to "keep the steam up and stand quietly where you are for a minute." Taking out his pocket watch, Jess waited for exactly four minutes, then said "OK, start the train moving again."

This time, he waited until the train had proceeded up the track for about two miles. Given the steep slope, the train was still moving quite slowly despite having travelled the two miles, at which point Jess simply said: "Good day," jumped off the locomotive and disappeared into the forest.

It took a moment for the engineer and fireman to recover from this latest surprise, after which they promptly stopped the train again and went to find the conductor. All three men realized that the train was being *robbed, and now they even knew how it was being done. Following a quick discussion, it was agreed that they would reverse the train and retrace the two miles they had just travelled.*

There was no reason to hurry.

***

While Jess had been busy in the locomotive, his partners had not been idle.

As soon as the train had been stopped, Jon and Slim had boarded it and hunched down over the link-and-pin coupling between the express car and the baggage car. The pin didn't want to come free but Slim had brought a crowbar with him, which he applied effectively. Despite the stuck coupling pin, this had only taken a little over three minutes. By four minutes, they had jumped off the train and were running to their next positions.

When the train restarted its ascent into the forest, the express car and the caboose were left standing alone at the edge of the clearing. By this time, Slim had taken up his position in front of the express car's big sliding door, while Jon had boarded the caboose to check for railway personnel. Finding two crew members in the caboose, Jon kept them in place at gunpoint. Like Jess, Jon had produced two large Colt double-action .45s. As the next few minutes ticked by, the two frightened crew members must have wondered what the stranger was waiting for. They soon found out, however, as a large, double explosion rang out.

At the express car, there was no attempt to order the guards that must certainly be present to open the big sliding door. Instead, Slim had simply dropped the crowbar he had been carrying and, taking several sticks of dynamite from a bag slung over his shoulder, affixed them along the lower edge of the door. He then lit the fuses and ran to take cover around the end of the car. He had just covered his ears with both hands when there was a double, thundering roar from the exploding dynamite.

The big, sliding door, being held in place only by its rollers along the top and double latches secured from the inside, was completely destroyed by the blasts. Splinters from the door were still falling from the sky as Slim ran back to the gaping doorway with, again, two large revolves drawn. Pointing and waving with his guns, he ordered the two shell-shocked guards to drop their rifles — which, in fact they had already done — and jump out of the car. Slim herded them to the caboose, and ordered them to join the two trainmen that were already being watched by Jon.

With Jon watching the four men in the caboose Slim returned to the express car, spent only a few minutes there, then jumped and once again took position to one side and put both hands over his ears.

Things were happening so quickly that the four captives in the caboose had only just realized what was coming next, when three explosions rang out in rapid succession.

When the dust settled, Slim re-boarded the express car carrying his crowbar. Moments later, canvas bags began to sail through the air, out the door, and down onto the ground beside the track. There were 13 bags in all, and a careful observer would have noticed that the bags were moderately heavy — about 10 pounds each - of which some made clinking sounds when they struck the ground, while others did not. The former were nine bags containing $5 and $10 gold coins from the Canadian Mint in Ottawa, while the latter were four mail sacks containing Dominion of Canada paper currency.

Once again, the process only took a few minutes after which Slim jumped down from the express car, placed two fingers into his mouth and gave a sharp whistle. This was a signal for the gang's three horses to come out of the forest and join them, which they did. Slim's whistle was also the signal for Jon to go and help load the horses, which he did after first leaving the men in the caboose with stern instructions to "stay put."

With Slim and Jon working together it took several more minutes to distribute the bags among the three horses and to tie Jess' horse behind that of Jon. After that, they picked up the guards' rifles, mounted up and rode off into the forest. As soon as they were out of sight, they made a sharp turn onto a game trail, rode just far enough to be out of sight of the tracks, then dismounted and prepared to wait.

It wasn't long before the rest of the train made its way slowly down the track, and the crew reconnected the cars. As the gang's leader, Jon, had predicted, the train then simply resumed its original journey up through the forest. Not being equipped to chase or deal with three heavily armed robbers, the crew had decided to continue to the next town where they could report the robbery and let the authorities deal with it.

When the train had passed them for the last time, Jon and Slim rode back down the game trail and then brazenly followed the path of the train — right up the tracks. Two miles ahead, they encountered a man sitting on one of the rails.

"Any trouble?" said Jess.

"None. You?" replied Jon.

"Nope," said Jess. Slim just gave a quiet smile.

Untying his horse, Jess mounted up and the three men rode off. Once again, they simply followed the tracks, but this time going the other way — heading west.

The gang hadn't bothered to wear masks because they were unknown in Canada and were planning to promptly leave the country. They were, in fact, headed for Vancouver where they would board a steamship heading south to the United States.

The whole episode took place so quickly and smoothly that it had either been meticulously planned and practiced, or they had done this before, or both. In only 45 minutes' time, the three men had stolen $44,000 comprising just over a thousand ounces of gold coins, worth $24,000, and paper currency comprising twelve thousand 25¢, $1, $2, and $5 bills worth $20,000.

Not everything went completely smoothly, however. Shortly after the three men entered the train tunnel, several shots rang out in the darkness.

One mile further along the track, a single man, on a single horse, rode out of the tunnel.

Knowing that an alert would be put out to watch for people trying to sell gold coins — which had become rare since the beginning of the 1914 world war - Jon planned to hide that part of the loot until it was safe to come back for it. Which might be never, he reflected, as he now had $20,000 in currency, which seemed like more than enough — especially since he no longer had to share it.

As for his former partners, Jon was reminded of a saying of his fellow American Benjamin Franklin[3]:

"Three may keep a secret, if two of them are dead."

The Daily News

Tuesday, August 3, 1920

Daring Train Robbery
Thieves Strike in Mountain Pass

Laurie Schramm

2 A CROSS-CANADA VENTURE

Day 1
May 26, 1978
Halifax, Nova Scotia
At the CN Rail Station

"All Aboard!"

Silver and I had been waiting to board VIA Rail's *Ocean* train at the Halifax South End Station. The progress of history was very much in evidence here. First, there was the station itself. This was Halifax's third train station, built in 1922 to replace its immediate predecessor the North Street station, which had been essentially destroyed in the Halifax Explosion of 1917[4]. Beside the station was the classic Hotel Nova Scotian and not far away was Halifax's famous Pier 21.

The current station reminded me of a museum to the age of steam locomotion. Its ornate, white-limestone exterior had an imposing sequence of tall columns. Passing through these into the station, you just had to stop and stare at the sheer size and grandeur of the Ticket Lobby, with its immense, arched ceiling and its huge expanse of information, ticketing, and baggage wickets plus benched seating areas, and innumerable side arches and doorways leading who knows where.

This would be a security nightmare, I thought to myself, imagining what it would look like in peak holiday season. So many people could be crowded into so much space, with so many entrances and exits. I remember thinking: *Looking for someone in here could be like looking for a needle in a haystack.*

The station was the eastern terminus for Canada's cross-country VIA Rail passenger trains, what the train people called a 'stub-end terminal.' Here, incoming trains would disembark their passengers and baggage, then locomotives and rail cars would be turned around on a turntable in preparation for their next departure.

When Silver and I had checked in and made our way to the departure area, the past and present came together in striking contrast. We were standing in the train shed, which was another massive structure – essentially a big roof that provided cover from the weather for the trains and passengers alike as they got on with the business of embarking and disembarking. This was no ordinary roof, however. It extended for some 1,500 feet south over the tracks and was supported by large, strong-looking steel pillars and cross-braces, all of them in a kind of dirty black. In addition to the feeling of space, the train shed felt dark and dirty, which it wasn't really, and damp, which it was – this was Halifax after all – and it felt old, which it certainly was. I say all this to underscore the contrast between the station we were in and the train we were about to board.

The train, in contrast, looked clean, modern, and new. It wasn't really all that modern and new. The Canadian government had just created VIA Rail as a Crown Corporation (meaning government owned) the year before and it had only been in the current year that the whole project had fully come together: a single, integrated passenger rail service that would span almost the full breadth of Canada. The locomotives and rail cars had all been acquired from the Canadian National (CN) and Canadian Pacific (CP) railways but had been cleaned-up and painted-over with the new VIA Rail livery, so that they looked new. Not only that, standing there in the literal shadow of the historic Halifax train station made them look almost futuristic.

It felt different to be in uniform for this trip. Granted, it was only my tactical uniform with a dark blue police-baseball cap, not the formal, red-serge tunic for which Mounties are famous. But so much of my work lately had been under-cover that being in uniform at all had become somewhat uncommon for me. Even Silver was wearing a police-service-dog vest.

Between me being a woman and Silver an Alaskan Malamute that looked remarkably like a large wolf, neither of us looked like most people's image of a Mountie. The same could not be said, however, for my colleague, Constable Jack McDonald.

Jack was tall, square-jawed, and handsome with an easy, outgoing disposition. If anything, he looked like the stereotypical Hollywood Mountie. Although he wasn't wearing his red serge, Stetson hat, and high boots, he did have on his yellow-banded forage cap, brown serge jacket with brown leather Sam Browne belt and holster, yellow striped pants and short boots. Even in his working ('Service Order') uniform, he wouldn't have looked out of place on a movie- or recruiting poster.

I don't want to give you the wrong impression, I liked Jack, and still do. We met in basic training[5] and had trained in the same troop together. Although he had a fearsome, and well-earned reputation as a womanizer, he had always treated me as a colleague – professionally and with respect. In the years since graduating, of the whole troop, it was Jack whose path I'd crossed most often. We'd worked well together on some dangerous assignments, and I'd learned that I could depend on him[6,7,8].

Perhaps I should back up a bit and tell you some of my story.

My name is Alexandra Houston. My friends call me Alex. Four years previously, in the summer of 1974, I'd been 24 years old, and feeling like my career was at a standstill. I'd studied chemistry at university and liked it, but not enough to pursue science as a career. I'd reset my sights on police work next, and had joined the Metropolitan Toronto Police force (Metro). Although policing seemed like a better fit for me than science, my two years with Metro had mostly comprised routine administrative- and traffic duties. These assignments were important, and needed to be done by somebody, and done well. But for me, they didn't fit the Hollywood vision of policing that I had developed, and I hadn't found them to be very challenging.

They say you should be careful what you wish for.

My life changed drastically with an unexpected meeting. Without explanation, my Captain had sent me to go and see a very senior Royal

Canadian Mounted Police (RCMP) officer. My reaction to this was apprehension, and I wondered what I could possibly have messed-up so badly that it had caught the notice of our national police force.

That's how I first came to meet Assistant Commissioner George MacLeod. After a lengthy conversation that I belatedly realized was an interview, he told me that he had asked my Captain (his friend) to recommend one of his young officers for a special pilot project he had in mind. He wanted someone who wanted to accomplish things, someone eager and tenacious, someone chomping at the bit to be allowed to do some 'real' police work, and... someone female. At this point he had shed his stern 'Mountie look,' relaxed his entire body, chuckled, and said that my Captain had recommended the "biggest pain in the butt" in his Division - me.

Assistant Commissioner MacLeod had explained that the 'Force' had fallen behind the times, and that its senior leadership wanted to build a more diverse police force. "We're going to be recruiting immigrants, visible minorities, maybe even people with some kinds of disabilities as well," he said, "But we have to start somewhere, and that somewhere is by engaging women." He wanted to try a first 'pilot test' with a woman, but that pilot test had to succeed as it would pave the way for an entire first troop of policewomen that would follow. He had thought of using someone that had already qualified as a policewoman, and simply re-train them in the 'RCMP way.'

That had brought me up to full attention. "Wait a minute! Do basic training all over again?"

"Yes!" he'd replied, "that's the only way you can possibly succeed. In the old days of the Northwest Mounted Police, a person could get appointed straight into the Force, even as a commissioned officer, if they had the right political connections. No more. Now everyone starts out the same way, as a Constable, and by going through the same basic training. If you want to have any hope of being accepted, much less respected, that's how you have to begin."

So, in the fall of 1974, I went through training at the RCMP's 'Depot' Division training centre in Regina, dealt with the good and the bad issues that came with being the first woman to train there, and survived to become the first woman Mountie. I hadn't intended for it to happen, really. The opportunity just came and found me.

After training, or re-training if you like, I'd been posted to Radium City, a small town in very northern Saskatchewan that, in its early days, had been a great uranium mining centre. Although my new boss, Corporal Morrison, had told me that nothing interesting ever happened around there, he'd been wrong, and I'd had to rescue him from a mine collapse, run our entire detachment single-handed while he was confined to hospital for six weeks, get rescued by a strange dog from near-death, solve a mystery, and find and catch a murderer – all in only four months!

The dog was named Silver. Investigating a mysterious series of break-ins had led me to some unusual places, including several abandoned uranium mines. In one such mine I'd fallen through a trap and found myself hanging precariously over the sharp edge of a vertical mine shaft. Unable to get out and tiring fast, I was saved by the almost magical appearance of what I first took to be a wolf, which gave me quite a scare, but turned out to be Silver, an Alaskan Malamute. Silver somehow sensed that I was in danger, had decided to help, and with his assistance I had been able to climb up and out of the raise. To make a long story short[5], while I'd continued to investigate the case, he had attached himself to me, was eventually given to me, and we'd been close friends ever since.

Sometime later I'd found myself in another surprise meeting with the same Assistant Commissioner MacLeod. Once again, a "coffee meeting" had turned into an interview and, once again, he had something new in mind for me. By this time, he'd become head of the Force's Security Service[9] and, unsurprisingly, he had some new ideas he wanted to try out by way of some experimental pilot projects. One of them involved me.

That had taken me to Ottawa, where I joined the Security Service. My new boss, Staff Sergeant Robert (Bob) Simpson, introduced me to the shady worlds of spies, counter-espionage, anarchists, and terrorists.

As a prelude to my first real Security Service assignment, Silver and I were sent to Innisfail, Alberta, to be trained as a police dog and handler team[6]. "If that dog is going to go everywhere with you, then we should get him trained too," Assistant Commissioner MacLeod had announced, on one of his periodic visits. Both Bob and the Assistant Commissioner had been interested in the possibilities presented by the first female 'Mountie,' especially undercover possibilities, and they were also interested in, and seemingly amused by, the notion of me having Silver along as a kind of side-kick, since he looked absolutely nothing like a police dog. That officially brought Silver into the Mounties too, and that's how my best friend became my partner.

Since then, we've had more hair-raising adventures together[7,8,10,11], and our destinies were firmly inter-twined.

***

"All Aboard!" the conductor repeated.

Silver and I moved toward the train, which was called *The Ocean*. There were a few seniors ahead of us, being helped onboard. As we waited, an elderly man in front of us turned, looked at me and my uniform, then Silver and his police-service-dog vest, and said "You're a real policewoman?"

"Yes, Sir," I replied.

"Huh! What will they think of next?" I must have looked a bit put out, because he quickly followed-up with "No offense intended. My name's Oliver Risk and this is my son Nathan."

"How do you do? My name's Alex Houston, and this is my partner Silver." I looked at Oliver Risk with interest because I thought that I knew who he was but had never seen him in person before. He was of medium height with silvery-grey hair, which receded back from an expanse of forehead, bushy grey eyebrows topping heavy jowls and a boxer's slightly flattened nose. His manner seemed a bit grumpy to me, possibly even surly, and I noticed that Silver rather pointedly ignored him completely, which was never a positive sign.

His son, Nathan Risk, provided quite a contrast to his father. The first thing I noticed was his wide, innocent-looking, blue eyes, and his infectious smile. These were well complimented by a full head of blonde hair that gave him something of the appearance of a California surfer. The next most striking thing about Nathan's appearance was that his clothes proclaimed his profession. He was wearing a white clerical collar with a blue shirt. Clearly a pastor or minister in a Protestant religion.

My thoughts were interrupted by Nathan taking his father's arm and saying: "Come on Dad, it's the 1970s now. Things are changing. Let's get on the train and get settled."

"I see you're still getting the same reaction from people," said my colleague Jack, who had been standing just behind me.

"Not as often as I used to," I replied. "I don't mind, as long as people are polite, and it still helps when I'm working undercover."

As Oliver and Nathan disappeared up the steps and into the train, we found ourselves face to face with the conductor, who gave us a casual salute and said "Good afternoon. Looks like you officers are on duty. Is there some kind of trouble?"

"No trouble," I said, "I'm Constable Houston, this is my colleague Constable McDonald, and this is my partner Silver. When you have a spare moment, we can explain why we're here."

"François Boucher," he said, offering his hand to shake – even to Silver, who promptly raised one paw for him. "I did hear something about you already," he paused and thought for a moment. "We'll be leaving at 1 pm exactly. Why don't you come see me after the 2:30 stop at Truro, eh? I'll have an hour free then."

"Sounds great, thank you," I replied.

"My office is in the first sleeping car behind the dining car. Look for a sign saying 'Conductor' on the door."

Saying "OK," we boarded the train and set off in search of our roomettes.

The train comprised several different kinds of cars. Behind the locomotive was a diesel-powered, generator-boiler car (to provide battery-electrical power and steam heating to the rest of the train), followed by a baggage car. Next came a dome car that had passenger seats on the upper level, a dining room on the main level, plus a kitchen, snack bar and lounge. Behind that was a dedicated dining car, with its own kitchen, followed by two sleeping cars, and then a regular passenger car. Bringing up the rear of the train was another dome car, this one with passenger seats on the upper level, and four roomettes, a bar and a panoramic lounge at the very end.

Jack and I each had our own two-person roomette in the second sleeping car. Just ahead of us, I noticed Oliver and his son Nathan going into their roomette, which was only a couple of doors down from us.

In their day-time configuration, the roomettes had two comfortable armchairs and a small private washroom. In their night-time configuration two single beds folded down to replace the chairs.

We agreed to allow some time to stow our carry-on bags and then meet for coffee in the forward dome car, which was called the 'Skyline.'

There wasn't much to unpack so, while Silver curled up on the floor, I mostly sat in one of the armchairs and looked contentedly out the large picture-window. There wasn't much to see while the train was standing in the rail yard, but I was greatly looking forward to watching the scenery as we made our way across the country. *The Ocean* would take us from Halifax to Montréal, then a corridor train would take us from Montréal to Toronto, and finally *The Canadian* would take us from Toronto to Vancouver – all-in-all, a distance of more than 4,400 km.

When the train jolted forward to begin the journey, it shook me out of my reverie and Silver and I went in search of a table in the Skyline Car. While we waited for Jack, I ordered two cups of coffee, which the attendant promptly delivered along with a bowl of water for Silver.

Jack and I knew each other well enough that we mostly just sipped our coffees and watched the scenery pass by. I liked the ocean views the best, beginning with the protected waters of the Bedford Basin.

Our first stop, Truro, was one of many brief stops which only allowed the few minutes needed for a few passengers to get on or off. If we wanted to get off, we were told not to stray beyond the platform or, after a single brief warning, the train would leave without us. Neither of us got up from our table and, sure enough, it was only a few minutes before the train was moving again. That made it time for us to visit the conductor.

We had no trouble finding him. One of the doors on the first sleeping car had a brass plate with the word 'Conductor' engraved in it. Just underneath that was a holder into which one could slide temporary nameplates. It held a black plastic nameplate with white letters giving the current conductor's name: François Boucher. The door was open, and we found François waiting and ready for us.

His office appeared to be a converted 3-person roomette. There was a small desk and chair, a small side-table, and two visitor chairs. Where there would normally have been an upper bunk, a basket shelf had been installed along the full length of the wall. This was filled with an assortment of boxes. *Files and supplies*, I guessed.

"Come in. Take a seat," said François, with a large smile and waving expansively. "Not as comfortable as the chairs in your roomettes I'm afraid, but at least they fit into this little office, eh?"

There was, in fact, room for Jack and I to sit down, but not much else. I was about to ask Silver to wait in the corridor, but he was way ahead of me, squeezing himself in and laying on the floor at our feet with his body resting partly across Jack and my boots.

François was quick. He had correctly interpreted the expression on my face and Silver's quick movements. "That's a smart dog you have there, eh? He doesn't want to miss a thing that one, and if you close the door for privacy he won't be left outside."

"You're right about both," I confirmed, "but I don't think we need to close the door. It doesn't matter if we're overheard."

Our preliminaries were interrupted by Silver himself, however. He had no sooner settled himself in front of Jack and I than his head went up and he scrambled to his feet, clearly sniffing and heading for where François was seated.

"Silver…" I cautioned.

"It's OK," said François immediately. "He smells the cat, eh?"

"The cat?"

"I have a cat named Cleo. She's not here right now but Silver has caught her scent. Come see." He motioned for us to stand up and look over his desk and, sure enough, there on the floor beside his office chair was a comfortable-looking cat bed and one of those double-bowls for water and cat food.

After thoroughly sniffing around the cat's bed Silver came back, gave an unamused snort, and lay back down in front of Jack and I.

"Sorry about that," I said.

"*Pas de quoi[12]*," said François with a broad smile. "She's a railway cat, eh? She prowls the whole train. Sometimes she sleeps in the generator-boiler car where it's warm. Sooner or later, you'll see her. If you spot an orange, black, and white calico cat that looks like she owns the train – that's Cleo.

"I'll try to make sure Silver doesn't give her any trouble," I promised.

"Don't worry, she's fast and she's acrobatic. The most he'll be able to do is make her jump, but he'll never catch her." Then, looking pointedly at Jack and I, he returned to our previous topic. "I was told about you. I'm supposed to help you if I can. You're here to look over security, eh? Anything I should be worried about?"

"No. Not at all. There's going to be a group of VIPs travelling this route later this year. Our job is travel with you and observe. Then we'll pass our notes up the line, and others will finalize the security arrangements for the VIP trip."

"OK. What are you supposed to observe?"

"Everything and anything," began Jack, who ran down a list of things we wanted to observe like the various stops, the facilities and terrain near the stops, the ease with which someone could slip onto the train unnoticed, and so on.

"That should keep you busy," commented François thoughtfully. "Let me show you something." He pulled out a copy of the train schedule covering the portion from Halifax to Montréal. "See here we have two 15 minutes stops, at Moncton and Sainte-Foy, plus 14 stops that are just long enough to get the odd passenger on or off, then 9 other places where we only stop if a passenger at the stop waves us down or if a passenger on the train comes and asks me. Plus, we can be stopped in many places to wait for a freight train to pass us."

We must have looked a bit disconcerted at this, because François chuckled and said: "Don't worry. Once you've watched a few of each kind of stop, they all look pretty much the same after that. Besides, if you have any questions about anything, come and see me."

"Thank you," said Jack, "that's great."

"Will you only be our conductor as far as Montréal?" I asked.

"Normally that would be the case, yes. But in this case, the answer is no..." He paused for effect. "I won't be with you on the corridor train between Montréal and Toronto, but we'll be together again on *The Canadian*, all the way to Vancouver. Very unusual, that is. But, it's the company's idea of being helpful – so you don't have to keep explaining yourself over and over when you change trains, eh?"

"That's great," I said, "I hope you don't mind?"

"Mind? I've been in a rut, eh? Travelling with *The Atlantic* back and forth, back and forth. This will make for some adventure. I'm going to enjoy it." He punctuated this with another brilliant smile, then: "So, if you don't have questions for me right now, how about if I take you on a tour of the whole train, eh?"

We said that would be great, and François took us to the dome car at the rear of the train, then we backtracked and went all the way to the front. The only locked door we encountered was that of the baggage car. As we passed through it, François recommended we leave Silver there as the next passageways would be very noisy. Leaving Silver, the three of us continued forward.

'Noisy' turned out to be an understatement, particularly as we walked along the narrow corridor that led to the front of the locomotive. Once we reached the cab, however, it was reasonably quiet and we were introduced to the engineer and shown the fantastic view that he had of the scenery and the rails and signals that lie ahead. The scenery changed to rivers and forests as we passed from Nova Scotia into New Brunswick.

François indicated that he wanted to remain up front and speak with the engineer so, after a last long look through the forward windows, Jack and I said our 'thank-yous' and headed back to collect Silver at the baggage car and return to our roomettes.

We hadn't been back to our roomettes for long before the train stopped in Moncton, New Brunswick. At 15 minutes, this was one of the longer stops so Silver and I went for a walk along the length of the train, pausing only to watch some baggage being loaded and unloaded for a few minutes. I took out my notebook and made a few notes on how easy it would be for someone to slip onto the train at such stops.

It certainly didn't look like it would be difficult for a stranger to slip on or off the train at any crowded station stop. The trick would be for someone to find a place to hide on the train itself, unless they could get a *bona fide* passenger to hide them in one of the larger roomettes.

Neither Silver nor I sensed anything concerning, although I thought that he looked a bit longingly at a snowshoe hare that had paused at the side of the railway property.

When the "all Aboard" call came, at 5:35 pm, we simply boarded the baggage car and walked back to our roomette via the inside corridor. It was already almost time for supper.

As we walked, I noticed that it wasn't very crowded on the train. Family vacations wouldn't begin for several more weeks yet, after schools recessed for the summer in mid-June. University students were out for the summer semester, however, and the passenger car was about half-full of university age students travelling coach class, meaning that they only had upright seats for the whole trip, although they could get up and walk around of course, or go to the bar and dining areas. Seeing the students brought back memories for me. As a university student, I had travelled that way myself once, from Saskatoon to Toronto and had found the trip exciting but exhausting - due to lack of sleep. I was glad I had a roomette this time.

Once again, Oliver and Nathan Risk were ahead of us when Silver and I entered the Dining Car. They were sitting alone. Nathan seemed to be doing all the talking, while Oliver simply stared out the window, seeming not to pay much attention to either his son or the scenery, which was shifting from lakes and farms into mostly forests and rivers.

I wasn't sure whether the staff would let Silver come with me to the dining section, but the attendant took it in stride and seated us as if it were an everyday occurrence. She did seat us at a table at one end of the dining section, commenting that it was to minimize any potential problems for people with allergies, but that was no problem for us. Another attendant simply removed one chair from our table so Silver could sit or lie down beside me. Not only were we able to eat together, but the staff made quite a fuss over Silver and the lady chef obviously appreciated the opportunity to prepare something out of the ordinary, as she came out first to meet us and make some suggestions. We had experienced something like this on a previous case[13], in which we travelled, twice, in a Canadian Navy Destroyer. There, the Navy chefs had made extravagant efforts to feed Silver in royal style. I certainly appreciated their efforts and I think Silver did too although, as a former sled dog, he could probably have eaten just about anything. Once again, I was contentedly enjoying the scenery pass by when Jack came to join us.

"I could get used to this kind of duty," he said, taking his seat across from me.

"Me too," I agreed. "I still find myself appreciating how nice it is to be warm again."

"You were up to something north of the Arctic Circle earlier this year, weren't you? Something to do with that Soviet satellite that crashed up there?"

"Yes, to both questions. Let's order our meals, then I'll tell you all about it." After the attendant took our orders and brought us coffee, I related my previous big assignment, in which I'd posed as a university scientist so I could join a team of specialists in their search for radioactive debris from a fallen Soviet spy satellite[11]. My underlying mission had been to watch out for Soviet agents that might also be on the team looking for a piece of secret new technology that might have survived. As we ate dinner, I related the story while trying to casually observe the other people that came into the dining car. This wasn't too difficult a task as I was facing the entire dining section, and only six other people came in to eat. Of those, only three struck me as being out of the ordinary.

The first two were an elderly man and a young woman who came and sat two tables ahead of us and on the same side of the train, which put them in the middle of the dining section and on the opposite side from Oliver and Nathan Risk. I knew who the man was: Colonel James Peters, a retired veteran of the Canadian Army with distinguished service in both the Second World War and the Korean Conflict.

He was the type of person that's hard to miss: tall and solidly built, ruggedly handsome with a square jaw and piercing blue eyes. He was showing his age a bit now, with greying hair, receding at the temples. *He must be about 75*, I thought, but he still retained the overtly military bearing of his former career, and still seemed to be quite fit and mobile.

I later learned from François that the young woman with him was his daughter, Hannah Peters. She certainly didn't look much like him. She was slender, almost willowy in build, of medium height, and had long, drab-blonde hair, and brown eyes that seemed to me to have a melancholy look. I guessed that she was probably about 18 years old. The two of them seemed to pass their dinner in companionable discussion, and the Colonel's quiet smiles, with their hint of mischievousness, made me think that the two of them were probably quite close. Unfortunately, I was too far away to hear anything.

The third person that caught my attention was another young man that I overheard asking specifically for the table that was just ahead of mine but on the other side of the train. When the attendant tried to seat him, he ignored the first seat proffered and sat himself so that he was facing towards the majority of the other tables. I would have put this down to a simple desire to face the same way that the train was heading - as some people find it uncomfortable to have their back to the direction of travel – except that, as dinner progressed, he seemed to be closely watching Oliver and Nathan Risk. Certainly, he spared an occasional glance at the scenery rolling by to one side, and also for the pretty Hannah sitting across the aisle and one table further ahead, but his gaze would always come back to rest on the Risks.

It seemed to me that Oliver Risk, in particular, was the focus of the young man's attention. Whenever Oliver spoke to his son – which wasn't very often – the younger man paid close attention, although I doubted that he was sitting close enough to overhear anything. I found out later, from François, that his name was Benjamin Shaw, that he was travelling alone, and that he was booked to travel with us all the way to Vancouver, as were the Risks, as were the Peters.

The plot thickens! I thought.

Silver

3 ONTARIO INTERLUDE

Day 2
May 27, 1978
Sainte-Foy, Québec

I awoke to the rising sun at 5 am. During the night, the train had continued to make its way through New Brunswick and would have crossed into the province of Québec shortly after midnight. The next brief stop would be in Sainte-Foy, a small city near the provincial capital: Québec City, so I had a bit of time to lounge in bed watching the scenery before getting dressed. I wanted to take Silver for another walk around the train when it stopped.

We had just enough time to make a complete circuit of the train. Passengers weren't allowed to walk around the far side of the train, but with Silver and I in uniform, no one bothered us. I didn't spot anything new or noteworthy on our circuit, but I made a show of writing notes in my notebook anyway, and then a sharp "All Aboard!" signaled that it was time for us to get back on the train.

Jack joined Silver and I for breakfast in the dining car and, since for a few minutes we were the only passengers dining, we were able to quietly 'talk shop.'

"How was your evening?" I asked Jack, knowing that he had planned to change into civilian clothes and spent some time in each of the coach, coffee shop, and bar sections of the train.

"Not bad," he replied. "There was a little excitement just before midnight when one of the passengers in the bar got pretty rowdy, and you could see that some of the others were worried he might turn violent. He was loud and obnoxious more than anything else though, so I just sat back and kept an eye on him. When we stopped in Campbellton, the CN Police[14] came on board and arrested him. There was a laugh-or-cry moment, when the man's wife tried to intervene. When that didn't work, she followed them all off the train, yelling and screaming at them the whole time. I suspect she may have had too much to drink as well.

Other than that, the main passenger car was like one big party. It was noisy too, but that was because a couple of the kids had brought guitars with them, and there was a lot of singing going on."

"I remember it being the same when I travelled in 'coach' as a teenager one summer. I gather they were better behaved than your drunk though?"

"Oh, sure. They seemed like a pretty good bunch, just having fun."

"I don't doubt it," I said, suddenly feeling a bit old.

"When I left, they were going strong and planning to party through the whole night," Jack continued. "No sign of anyone of special interest." That meant he hadn't seen Oliver Risk or the Colonel.

For my part, I had left Silver behind, changed in to civilian clothes, and spent time in each of the upper-deck vista domes and other small lounge areas. "The domes were quiet," I reported. "It was sightseers until sunset, and then it seemed to be people in coach class that wanted to find a quiet place to sleep for the night. I didn't see anyone of special interest either, so it looks like they kept to their roomettes."

After breakfast, the three of us took an inside stroll along the full length of the train and back, returning to our roomettes to re-pack our carry-on bags as the train crossed the St. Laurence River prior to pulling into the station at Montréal. Arriving at 10:15 am put us only a few minutes late, leaving us time to walk around the station.

While I had the opportunity, I stopped at the first pay phone I encountered and placed a collect call to my boss, Staff Sergeant Bob Simpson in Ottawa. He wasn't there, but I left a message with a duty officer providing a brief description of Benjamin Shaw and asking for any information they could find on him.

Silver and I then boarded the corridor train that was scheduled to depart for Toronto at 11 am. The corridor trains, being mostly for commuters and not travelling overnight, only had coach cars so we took a spot at one end of the car where two bench seats faced each other, with a table in-between them. I sat on the side facing the length of the car, but positioned myself so I could watch people as they entered, and we settled in.

Within minutes I was treated to an interesting procession. First came Oliver and Nathan Risk, the former looking a bit grumpy – again – and walking slowly. Nathan Risk, again wearing his clerical collar, had a supportive hold on one of his father's arms, and a sunny expression on his face. He held a thick book in his other hand, just like he'd had when we first met, and it dawned on me that it was probably a bible - part of his standard equipment.

Behind the Risks were a cluster of business people, all of them wearing suits, looking very focused, and carrying briefcases. Next, came the Peters. Once again, the Colonel exuded a purposeful military bearing that contrasted sharply with the carefree, fluid movements of his daughter Hannah. I noticed with interest that the Colonel again chose seats that were somewhat behind, and across the aisle from, the Risks.

Next came another cluster of business people and briefcases, followed by Jack. Silver was lying on the bench seat across from me, so when Jack turned to join us, I quietly patted the seat beside me. That gave him the same view down the length of the car, and I leaned towards him and whispered: "All parties of interest are further up the car. Do you want to place a bet on whether our mystery person sits behind them?"

I never found out what Jack thought because I'd no sooner whispered the words when Benjamin Shaw stopped right beside us and carefully scanned the disposition of the car ahead of us. After a moment's hesitation he took a seat facing forward that was on the same side of the car as the Risks but behind both the Risks and the Peters. If I'd had any doubts the day before about his presence on the train being coincidental, there were no doubts any longer and I was glad that I'd put the request for information through to my boss before boarding.

The trip from Montréal to Toronto was relatively short, being scheduled for five and a half hours. We very quickly passed from Québec into Ontario, and people mostly sat in their seats and looked out the windows or, in the case of the business-people, read newspapers or read and scribbled notes on important-looking files.

There was a service counter in our car, from which people acquired lunch or snacks, but not in any particular pattern that I could discern. Near the mid-point of our trip there was a brief stop at the Kingston Station, but Silver and I were virtually the only ones to take advantage of the opportunity to stretch our legs and, in his case, heed the call of nature.

As the journey unfolded, I tried to inconspicuously keep an eye on the Risks, Peters, and Benjamin Shaw but, from my vantage point at least, it was a re-run of the previous evening's action. Oliver Risk seemed to moodily look out the window, Nathan Risk seemed immersed in reading his book or bible, the Colonel and his daughter gave every appearance of two people enjoying a father-daughter vacation, while Benjamin reminded me of a hawk watching its prey. The one difference from the previous evening was that Benjamin seemed to be more frequently distracted by the presence of Hannah Peters.

This is starting to feel like a movie drama, I thought.

We arrived in Toronto at 4:30 pm and disembarked into Union Station. This is another classic structure, reminiscent of Halifax's train station but much larger! Jack and I collected our checked bags and walked across the street to the Royal York Hotel, where we'd be staying for the night. The Royal York was another experience in living history. Built by the Canadian Pacific Railway Company (CP) in 1929, it is one of Canada's more than twenty historic, grand 'railway hotels' which, whether built by CN or CP, stretch from St. John's, Newfoundland to Victoria, British Columbia. The first sensations I had when entering the hotel were the early-20th century architecture and décor, the size of everything, and the quiet. Despite the number of people going about their business on the expansive first floor, once the doors swung shut behind us the sounds of the busy downtown were sealed out and a hush descended around us.

While we were checking in, we asked the concierge if there might be a chance of getting a reservation in the revolving restaurant of the CN Tower, which was only a few blocks away. He said he'd see what he could do and would call us.

Although the hotel was a classic – in other words: very old – it had gone through several renovations in the previous six years and our rooms were quite modern, but still furnished and decorated to match the hotel's long-standing character. Here too, the rooms were extremely comfortable looking, and extremely quiet.

I had no sooner dropped my bags on the floor and looked around my room than the phone rang. It was Jack calling to say that the concierge had phoned, and we could have a table for two if we could get to the tower by 5:30, otherwise they were fully booked for the evening. Jack said the concierge had also cautioned that, unless we were on official duty, Silver wouldn't be allowed in. Agreeing to go right away, I changed into casual clothes, put a bowl of water out for Silver and left him to wait in the room while I went down to the lobby to meet Jack.

Reaching the lobby, I found that Jack was there ahead of me and sitting in a large leather easy chair: the comfortable type that is both mentally and physically difficult to get out of. As I approached, I expected him to get up right away but he surprised me by just sitting and looking at me. When I was close enough, he used a very soft voice to say: "Take a moment, and then casually glance over to your right."

Hesitating as I took this in, I slowly turned to my left and swept my gaze around the whole lobby area, as if taking in the architecture. As my gaze came nearly full circle, I saw what Jack had. About thirty feet away, three people were just meeting, and then walked out of the lobby together as if heading for a night on the town. It was Nathan Risk, with no clerical collar this time, Hannah Peters, and Benjamin Shaw.

"Looks like the young people are getting acquainted," said Jack.

"Young people!" I said, "you're making me feel old." I was about to turn 28 that summer, and not at all prepared to think of myself as being old. I estimated that Jack was four or five years younger than me as he had joined the Force within a year of graduating from high school, whereas I had gone to university and then spent two years with the Toronto City Police before joining the Force.

Chuckling, Jack levered himself out of his chair and said: "Want to try following them?"

"No. I think we should lie low. Let's go out on the town ourselves."

As I mentioned, the CN Tower was only a few blocks from our hotel and a pleasant stroll took us to the tower and the elevator that whisked us to the top. I was looking forward to the view. Construction of the tower had just begun when I left Toronto to join the Force, and I hadn't been back to Toronto since it was completed and opened in 1976.

Our table was right beside the expansive glass windows, and we had to tear our eyes away from the scenery to look at the menus and decide what to order. The backs of the menus explained that the CN Tower was the world's tallest free-standing structure (at that time), and the equivalent of a 147-story building, standing 457 m (1,500 ft) to its roof, and 553 m (1,815 ft) to the top of its antenna spire.

Luckily for us, it was a clear evening and as our dinner progressed it made a complete revolution. Since the tower stood about four blocks from the shore of Lake Ontario, we had great views of the lake and shoreline for about half of the time, and of the mass of downtown high-rises for the other half. Beyond sight-seeing, we avoided talking about work and just had a nice, relaxing dinner.

It was still nice outside after dinner and I wanted to go collect Silver for a stroll along the waterfront. Jack wanted to come too, so we went back to the hotel for Silver and then took a long walk along the lakeshore. Being a Saturday night, there were plenty of people out for walks, going to waterside bars and restaurants, and taking harbour cruises.

For a few moments here and there, it was easy to forget that we were on a mission but the mission - a mission within a mission, really – was never very far from our thoughts.

The next morning we'd be boarding another train, and I remember wondering whether it was all going to be just a big waste of time.

It wasn't.

4 *THE CANADIAN*

Day 3
May 28, 1978
Toronto, Ontario

It was a windy and rainy Sunday in downtown Toronto when Silver and I took an early morning walk along the lakeshore. There was no message from my boss, Bob, yet but I knew that it could take some time for them to get the information I asked for.

After checking out of the hotel and meeting up with Jack, we walked across the street, checked in with VIA Rail, and boarded *The Canadian* for its 09:45 departure.

The train pulled out of Union Station on schedule. I noticed that it had a few more cars than we'd had on *The Ocean*, but our car seemed to have the same passengers as before, and with their roomettes in the same corresponding positions.

Not long after leaving the outskirts of Toronto the weather improved just as we began to cross the Canadian Shield, with its lakes and forests. As we continued along, rocky outcrops began to appear more and more frequently, and I knew that as we approached Northern Ontario, we'd be seeing more and more rock. Although there were periods of heavy forest, these only made for a greater contrast when everything opened up as we crossed various waterways on old-looking railway bridges.

It's not uncommon for people to fall into habits like sitting in the same seats for school or university classes, and a similar thing had happened for many of the passengers when we were on *The Ocean* train. Things started to change on *The Canadian*, however. When Silver and I went to the dining car for lunch, we were again seated at one extreme end of the section, but this time some of the other passengers changed their seating arrangements. Oliver Risk and the Colonel were nowhere to be seen, and Hannah had initially sat down alone. She was soon joined, however, by Nathan and Benjamin, who came in together and were already in the midst of some kind of religious debate. Nathan was clearly back 'on duty,' wearing his clerical collar. As the three young people were sitting at the table right next to us, I could see that the book Nathan carried around when 'on duty,' was in fact a bible.

They're starting to get to know each other, I thought.

When Jack came to join us, sitting across the table from me and with his back to the next table he raised his eyebrows, signifying that he had also noticed the change in pattern. I nodded in turn, and settled in to listen and observe. I had no trouble overhearing, but the direction of the conversation threw me at first.

Nathan was saying to Benjamin: "Look Ben, I know it would be convenient, but no one gets to see God. The Bible says '*No one has ever seen God*,' John 4:12, and '*No man has seen or can see God*,' Timothy 6:16."

"That can't be right though," argued Ben. "Adam and Eve saw God, right? And in Genesis it says that God appeared to Abraham while he was sitting near his tent at Mamre, right? And in Exodus it says that God spoke to Moses, right?"

"That's right, how did you know?"

"I was dragged to a lot of Sunday-School Classes and they gave us tests. Since I was stuck in them anyway, I did the work and won some prizes for scripture knowledge. But you didn't answer my question."

"I think we're both right. God spoke to a very few people for specific reasons, but I think the general teaching is that no one should expect to be able to see God just because they want to."

"OK, but…"

As the debate continued, Jack raised his eyebrows and we shared a glance. Taking out my pen, I wrote a few words on a paper napkin and passed it across the table. *I think the boys are starting to compete for Hannah's affections*, it said.

Jack's eyes widened in understanding, then he nodded and passed the napkin back. Nathan and Ben's argument wasn't the least bit interrupted by the arrival of their food and they continued their verbal game throughout lunch. I had a clear view of Hannah's face during this time, and noted that she seemed bored, only half-listening as she ate and watched the rolling scenery out the window. I decided that I would look for an opportunity to engage her in casual conversation as soon as I could.

As it turned out, the opportunity dropped into my lap a few hours later. I'd been sitting with Silver in the Skyline Car, which was one of two dome cars on the train. We'd been up there for a while already: even Silver had been interestedly looking out the dome windows as the changing scenery rolled past. The observation levels in both dome cars tended to be full during daylight hours, and when Hanna came up the stairs looking for a seat, almost everything was already occupied.

Catching her eye, I waved her over and asked Silver to move from the double seat he'd been sprawled across to sit beside me. The freed-up seats faced mine and Silver's, separated by a small table. With a huge sigh, she flopped down on the seat facing me and dropped her huge purse on the seat beside her.

"Thank you," she said, "my name's Hannah."

"Pleased to meet you Hannah, my name is Alex and this is Silver."

"I saw you and your dog in the dining car on the train from Halifax, are you going to Vancouver as well? You're a Mountie, right? And a dog handler? Are you on duty?"

That was the most words I'd ever heard her say, but I didn't want to dampen her willingness to talk, so I tried to answer all of her questions.

"It's because you're on duty that they let a dog into the dining room, right?"

"That's right, and it's a real treat for Silver because the chef is spoiling him rotten."

She chuckled. "Can I pet him?"

"Let's find out. Try extending your hand so he can give it a good sniff, and look into his eyes."

That wasn't the answer she was expecting, so when she got up to reach over, it was a very tentative hand that she extended. Silver stretched his nose out a bit and gave it a good sniff.

"Now what?" she asked.

"Look at his body language. Does he look like he'd be OK with a friendly pet?"

"I think so," she said hesitantly, "I'm not sure."

"Trust me, if he didn't want you to get closer, you'd know. Go ahead, just do everything slowly so you don't surprise him."

Reaching her hand out further, she gave him a cautious rub behind one ear and her eyes opened wide. "He's leaning in to my hand."

"That's because you picked a good spot. He'd have been fine if you just patted him on the head, but he loves having his ears rubbed."

Sitting contentedly back in her seat, she smiled. It was the first time I'd seen her smile and the change from her usual melancholy was startling. Silver must have thought so too, because he immediately got up, switched seats, and laid down beside her, with his head on her leg.

"Looks like you've made a friend," I said, as she went back to rubbing behind one of his ears.

"I guess so," she said, sounding surprised. "I thought police dogs were trained to be vicious?"

"Not vicious, just trained to respond appropriately to different circumstances."

Sensing an opportunity, I decided to try a little gentle probing. "Is that your father you're travelling with?"

"The Colonel? Yes. We're doing a father-daughter trip across the country." She must have seen the look of surprise on my face, and added: "Yes, everyone calls him Colonel – it's who he is and what he is."

"Well, it sounds like a nice idea to me. Aren't you interested?"

"Oh, yes. I wasn't at first because it came up so suddenly and he wasn't very nice about it. Last week, from out of nowhere he said we'd should do a cross-Canada train trip together and we'd be driving to Halifax and leaving on Wednesday... Just like that. As if he was giving order to one of his soldiers. Anyway, now that we're here, I'm actually enjoying it, so it turned out to be a good idea after all."

"How about the two admirers you seem to have attracted?"

That brought a blush to her cheeks. "Boys!" she said, dismissively. "Nathan and his dad are doing the same thing: a father-son cross-Canada trip to celebrate his graduation from divinity college."

Interesting coincidences, I thought. I knew the most likely reason that Oliver Risk was taking the trip. Now I had some insight into the reason for the timing, although I didn't expect it to help me much. I was tempted to risk prying a bit more, but was forestalled by a sharp voice coming from the stairwell.

"Hannah!"

"Oops, that's the Colonel bellowing. Have to run. Thanks for letting me pet Silver," she said, rising and picking up her purse.

"You're welcome. It was nice to meet you."

She leaned over while making her way around Silver and out into the aisle. "I don't think I'm supposed to be talking to you actually. Dad doesn't approve of women in the military and I'm pretty sure he feels the same way about women in the police."

"I'll try not to corrupt you too much," I whispered.

That prompted a giggle as she waved and went to join her father.

I decided to leave the dome level as well, and when the train pulled into the station for a half hour stop at Capreol, Ontario – which is near Sudbury - we took the opportunity to take a stroll around the train and the station. In both cases, I let Silver roam and sniff around as he pleased, while I scribbled inconsequential notes in my notebook.

At the baggage car, we went in and I had Silver search for explosives. I didn't expect there to be any, but I wondered how long it would take him to search the car when it contained so many pieces of luggage, each with their own set of scents. It took longer than I expected.

While we were in the station, I also took a few minutes to use a pay-phone to call my boyfriend Don who, fortunately, was at home in Halifax. Don was a Captain in Military Intelligence. We had met on a particularly hazardous assignment[7] and had since shared several others together[8,11]. Each shared assignment seemed to draw us closer together, although it had remained a long-distance relationship since I was based out of Ottawa.

It was nearly 6 pm when the train left Capreol: dinnertime.

When I went to see if Jack was ready for dinner, he wasn't feeling very hungry. "I spent some time looking over the food and bar preparation areas and talking to the staff there. I'm no health inspector, but everything looked proper to me and I made notes on their routines. While I was there, the chef and bartender insisted on feeding me samples, though, so I'm doing fine."

So, it was just Silver and I taking our accustomed places in the dining car. After a few minutes, Oliver entered and took his customary table, followed a few minutes later by the Colonel, who did the same. It was some time later, and most of us early diners were well into our entrées, when the three young people arrived – together.

Their voices preceded them, and even before seeing any of them I could hear Nathan's voice. "But Matthew said: '*whosoever shall smite thee on the right cheek, turn to him the other also,*' chapter 5, verse 39."

"Very noble," sneered Ben, "but in Exodus it says: '*and if any mischief follow, then thou shalt give life for life, eye for eye, tooth for tooth, hand for hand, foot for foot, burning for burning, wound for wound, stripe for stripe.*'"

That brought them to a halt, right beside my table, as Hannah exclaimed: "*Eewww,* how horrible. You shouldn't need a bible to tell you that's wrong."

Ben just angrily stared at both of them, and I could feel the tension rising between the three of them. The tension was broken, however by the one person I thought might be the most dogmatic: Nathan. "I can't tell you what the right answers are Ben. All I can do is give you some alternate perspectives. In the end, you have to make up your own mind what to believe."

That took the wind out of Ben's sails, as he was clearly expecting a rebuke, or at least an argument. Whatever his reply was, it was lost as the three of them moved along. Nathan went further ahead to join his father. Hannah, for her part, seemed to hesitate, then made a show of inviting Ben to sit with her and her father, the Colonel.

I tried to hide a smile. Ben was either trying to shake Nathan's faith or win the war of words. I suspected both, having now seen his temper flash. I couldn't tell whether Nathan was Pollyanna-like naïve or very smart, but either way he was proving to be up to the challenge of sparring with Ben.

There were no further episodes or outbursts during dinner.

Hannah and Ben seemed to engaged in casual conversation with her father while, further up the car, Nathan seemed to eat in silence while his father, Oliver Risk, simply ate and moodily stared out the window again.

Silver and I, for our part, had a great dinner. Each day's menu had several options to choose from and I was pleasantly surprised to find that the dining car meals were consistently very good. The dining car chef had once again created a 'daily special' for Silver, which he promptly devoured. Besides keeping a weather-eye on the travelers ahead of me and having lots of scenery to enjoy, François even dropped by for a friendly chat and a cup of coffee when we were finishing up. While I had his attention, I asked about how easy it would be for someone to stop the train.

"Simple," he replied. "Anyone can stand by the tracks and raise their arms above their head to indicate danger ahead, or they can wave a red flag, or at night wave a red light toward the train. But the train doesn't stop right away, eh? It can take a mile before it stops."

"How about from inside the train?"

"Well, someone can pull one of the emergency-brake handles in the cars. When that happens, it releases pressure in the brake lines, which puts the brakes on. Even then, the engineer can use an override control to keep the brakes off until they find a safe place to bring the train to a stop."

"Have you had people try to stop the train before?"

"Oh sure. Sometimes it's a drunk in the bar, or a crazy person on the tracks, but not often. The company gets upset, and the penalties are stiff, eh?"

"Hmmm," I said, scribbling in my notebook.

"Don't worry," he said, "it's very unlikely to happen."

Later in the evening, Silver and I were sitting in the upper level of the rear dome car when I saw François come up the stairs with a worried expression on his face.

Uh oh, I thought. Sure enough, he saw us and came straight over.

"Could I talk to you for a moment please?" he said, with a tip of his head indicating that we go somewhere else.

"Of course," I replied, and we followed him down the stairs and forward several cars until we reached his office. This time, he closed the office door when we were inside.

"One of the passengers is complaining that their roomette has been broken into."

"Really? How and when?"

"They say it must have been while they were in the Skyline Dome Car, where they went to wait while the attendant set up their sleeping berths for the night."

"They?"

"Mr. Risk and his son."

"Ah... and what was taken?"

"That's the crazy thing. Nothing was taken, eh?"

"How do they know their room was broken into then? Were things broken, stuff scattered around?"

"Nothing like that. Apparently when they returned to their roomette, they noticed that a few things had been moved from where they left them."

"Could it have been the attendant cleaning up?"

"No. Some of the things that were moved were files and documents in Mr. Risk's briefcase, and they swear that things were rearranged in their carry-on luggage."

"And the attendant?"

"Has been with the company for years. I knew him way back when we worked for CN, long before VIA Rail was created."

"Hmmm... and which of the Risks came to tell you about it?"

"The younger one, Nathan Risk. He was very upset. Why?"

"Just curious. What did Oliver Risk have to say?"

"He was mostly angry that the roomettes can't be locked from the outside. I told him that I can put any valuables he might have in a safe until we reach Vancouver, but he says they don't have anything valuable with them."

I considered this for moment, then, "OK. It doesn't sound like much of a crime has been committed, then. What would you like me to do?"

"I'd like to reassure them that we are taking this seriously. Would you come and talk to them; take a look at the roomette?"

"Sure. Lead the way."

François led us to our sleeping car and knocked on the door, which was opened by Oliver Risk.

"Now what?" he said.

"Would you please show Constable Houston the things that were rearranged?"

Oliver Risk wasn't in an accommodating mood. "Why?" he

growled, "I told you nothing was taken. We just want our privacy, that's all. If you want to do something constructive, put a lock on this door."

"Hi Mr. Risk," I tried. "We're very sorry to bother you, but the Conductor is very distressed about this, and he's asked me to take a look. I don't know whether there's anything we can do to help or not, but would you please just show us what was moved? It will only take a moment and then we'll leave."

Oliver hesitated a moment, and then seemed to judge that it would be the fastest way to get rid of us. "Come in then, if you must," he said ungraciously, and then showed me things in their carry-on bags that weren't in their usual positions and papers in his briefcase that weren't out of place, exactly, but not as neatly arranged as usual – as if someone had taken papers out, looked them over, and then hurriedly stuffed them back into their folders."

"And nothing was actually taken?" I asked.

"No. That's what I keep saying. Just some snoopy-drawers looking for valuables, but they didn't get anything."

"All right. Thank you," I said. "In that case, I don't think you'll be disturbed again. If we have a thief onboard, they'll go try someone else next time – if there is a next time. In the meantime, please let the conductor or I know if you remember anything missing. Good night."

"Good night!" he said, grudgingly.

As I made to leave the roomette, I happened to turn my head and look back as Oliver was bent over, closing up his briefcase. Reflected in the window I could see that there was a smirk on Oliver's face that he thought no one would be able to see.

There IS something to find, but it hasn't been found yet, I thought.

Motioning to François, I went and opened the door to my roomette. He was scandalized at the thought of being seen in a single woman's roomette but agreed to stand in the open doorway.

"Could I have a word with the attendant from this car?"

"Of course, come to my office in five minutes, eh?"

When Silver and I appeared at François' office at the appointed time, Émile Cournoyer, the attendant for our car was sitting in one of the chairs. We had previously met when he changed over my roomette, so I launched straight in. "Did you see the things that the Risks' say were rearranged?"

"Of course, but I didn't do anything or take anything."

"The things they say were moved, were they like that when you set up the berths for the night."

I didn't mean for it to be a trick question, and I don't think Émile even realized the trap as he simply answered that he didn't open any baggage or the briefcase, so there was no way for him to know.

"So, we don't know whether the intruder came before or after you then," I said.

"After," he said, positively. "The briefcase was in the right place, but the order of the two bags had been reversed. When I did the room, the black bag was to the left of the brown bag, but when François called me back to the room later, the black bag was on the right."

"You're sure?"

"Very sure."

"That's helpful, thank you. And did you see anyone or anything unusual in the car after you did the Risk's roomette?'

"No nothing at all… just the nun."

"The nun?"

"Yes. I'd just come out of doing one of the other rooms, when I saw a nun walking towards the end of the car."

"What did she look like?"

"Her back was facing me, so I couldn't see her face, but she was wearing a full black habit with one of those little caps on her head."

"Is that all you noticed about her?"

"Yes… no, wait. She was tall for a nun. Six feet at least."

François then asked Émile a few questions but it all came back to the same thing, he had seen the back of an unusually tall nun walking out of the sleeping car at about the right time, and no one else until later, when several of the passengers began returning to their roomettes.

François thanked him and Émile left to return to his duties. When he was gone, I noticed that François had a quiet smile on his face.

"What?" I asked.

"You are going to ask me about the nuns on the train, eh?"

"Yes, of course. Can you give me a list of names and whether they are travelling coach, or in berths or roomettes?"

"Certainly." His smile broadened. "There are no nuns on the train!"

"What? Are you sure?"

"Well, certainly there are none wearing formal habit. I have been up and down the full length of this train many times since we left Toronto. A nun in full habit I would have noticed. A six-foot-tall nun would stand out, eh?"

"So. Someone in disguise then… I think Silver and I will take a stroll along the train…" I saw the look in François' eyes. "No, I believe you. I'm not looking for nuns, I'm going to look for a discarded nun's habit. Would you ask the attendants to do the same, especially in the public washroom and shower areas?"

"Of course."

"Shoes too," I reflected. "Especially elevator shoes."

That prompted another chuckle. "I'll tell everyone right now."

Thanking him, Silver and I went to the rear of the Park Dome Car, at the back of the train, and slowly walked forward. As we went, I tried to glance at trash cans and the like without being too obvious about it. Along the way, we encountered Jack and I'd taken him aside and filled him in on what had happened.

Moving along, I got a shock in one of the upper-and lower-berth combinations that the railway called 'sections.' By day, these comprised open-plan, facing bench seats. In the evening, an attendant would arrange the two seats together and cover them with a mattress to make a lower berth. Above that, an upper berth would be hinged down from above. The evening arrangements would then be completed by attaching a short ladder to the upper berth, and attaching heavy curtains to each bunk for privacy.

In the car I was walking through, some of the sections had been set up for the night, while others were still in their seating configuration. As I passed one of the made-up sections, I noticed that the upper berth had a big lump under the blankets. It was the size lump that a balled-up nun's habit could make, and the section was unoccupied at the time, so I pulled up the top of the blankets to see what was underneath.

"*EEEAAAARRRRIR!*"

I was so startled that my subconscious immediately took over. As I let go of the blanket and pulled my arm back, a blur of orange, black, and white flew off the berth and vanished down towards the far end of the sleeper car.

"Silver!" I called, sharply, as I sensed him tensing to spring forward. "Stay! Let the cat go."

"*Eerrrr,*" he said, fighting down his instinct to chase the cat.
We had just met the conductor's cat, Cleo.

When my heart rate came down from hyper to just elevated, Silver and I continued our prowl through the rest of the train. It took a while, and when we finally reached the baggage car, the door was securely locked and didn't seem to have been tampered with. It had been a long shot, but I still felt discouraged. I had no further clues, no discarded disguise, and I hadn't seen any nuns either.

When Jack and I met up later on, I told him about our episode with Cleo the cat. Jack, of course, thought it was hilarious and didn't try to hide his grin as he related the news of his own scan of the train. Basically, he hadn't noticed anything out of the ordinary either.

We decided there wasn't anything more to be done for the time being, and said good night.

An hour later, I was in my bunk and still trying to get to sleep when there was a knock on the door. It was François. When I unlocked and opened the door, he refused to come in but he had a mischievous twinkle in his eyes. "We found something!" he said, raising a double armload of tangled black cloth."

"The nun's habit!" I exclaimed, as quietly as I could. "Where did you find it?"

"When the train stopped at Gogama, one of the attendants noticed something fluttering in the wind near the back of the Park Car. He called me and we went to have a closer look. Someone must have thrown it out a window further up the train, and instead of blowing away it got caught on one of the handholds bolted to the side of the car. It's where you climb up when you need to replace a burned-out bulb from the lights that face backwards along the track. So another train doesn't run into us in the night eh? It got caught there and wrapped around so tight, the wind couldn't dislodge it. Took us a while to get it off, but here it is."

"Can I hang onto it for a while?" I asked.

"You can have it. It's just garbage to us eh?" François handed over the habit, along with a plastic bag he'd thought to bring along, and I gave it a quick look-over to see if there were any identifying labels or markings. There weren't, and I stuffed the habit into the bag and thanked François for finding a good clue.

There's a pattern here, I thought.

5 CROSSING NORTHERN ONTARIO

Day 4
May 29, 1978

Once again, I awoke to the rising sun at 5 am. During the night, the train had continued to make its way through Northern Ontario. The sky was clear, and I knew that we would be in store for a cheerful morning of alternating forest and waterway views.

After getting dressed, I took advantage of the next brief stop to give Silver a chance to heed the call of nature. This turned out to be a five-minute stop at Longlac a small, appropriately named town on the shore of Long Lake. Then, it was on to breakfast. This being our second day on *The Canadian*, and the fourth day for those of us that had embarked in Halifax, most people had settled into vacation mode. As a result, there were very few people in the dining car for breakfast.

While I was eating breakfast, François joined me for a few minutes and had a cup of coffee for himself. I told him about our meeting with his cat, Cleo, the previous day, which amused him greatly.

"She pops up now and again, eh? You'll probably see her again before the trip is over." Then he turned serious and asked: "What do you think about the break-in? There's some kind of intrigue going on, I think. Maybe something that involves the police?"

I could tell that it worried him, and I wasn't surprised that he might be starting to suspect Jack and I of having an ulterior motive for being on the train."

"Maybe," I said, noncommittally. "Jack and I will try to keep an eye out for trouble and will let you know if we see anything that could affect the safety or security of your passengers."

That seemed to satisfy him for the moment, and our discussion shifted to less weighty matters. Somehow, we discovered that we shared an interest in SCUBA diving, he having grown up diving in quarries in Québec and having originally planned to go to university and become a fisheries biologist. He never got away from the railroad once he'd started working summer jobs there, which then led to full-time railroading, and then promotions led to becoming a locomotive engineer and, finally, a conductor. "It's in the blood now. That and being part of a huge family of colleagues, and the travel…," he sighed. "I won't leave it now until retirement time comes and they push me out, eh?"

After breakfast, I decided to take a chance and see if there was any available space on the upper viewing deck of the Park Dome Car at the rear of the train. Surprisingly, it wasn't very crowded. *People must be sleeping-in this morning,* I thought. It was easy to lose track of days on the train. For those of us that had taken *The Ocean* train leaving Halifax at 1 pm on Friday and taken the most efficient connections from Montréal to Toronto and boarded *The Canadian,* it was now our fourth day of travel.

Although there were quite a few seats available, I noticed Nathan sitting alone and, sensing an opportunity, I made a beeline for him.

As we approached, it became obvious that he wasn't exactly sitting alone. Curled up in his lap was the conductor's cat, Cleo.

"May we join you?" I asked, when we were close enough.

"Of course," he said, looking up and waving in the direction of the seats facing his.

Motioning for Silver to jump up on the seat beside me I said, warningly, "Leave the cat alone, Silver."

"*Eerrrr?*" he said, doing his best to look innocent.

"I've never seen such a well-behaved dog before," said Nathan, continuing to pet Cleo, who hadn't moved but was clearly watching Silver with untrusting eyes. "He really listens to you, doesn't he?"

"Most of the time, yes. We've become very close over the past few years.

"My name's Alex, and this is Silver."

"How do you do? My name's Nathan." Then he pointedly looked at my uniform, then directly into my eyes… "I guess neither of us has to identify our profession."

Despite his direct gaze, I found his manner to be unusually open and unoffending. *Innocent, almost,* I thought. "I guess not," I smiled.

"And both of us chose professions so we could help people, right?"

"Well, yes, but in my case, I also wanted something that would involve adventure."

"Do you get much adventure? I would have thought that policing is mostly just routine these days. Catching people speeding, handing out parking tickets, that kind of thing?"

"It was like that at first, but these last few years I've had enough scary adventures to make me realize that I should be careful what I wish for," I said, somewhat ruefully. But I wanted to try to steer the conversation back to him. "What about you? Are you actually on duty too?"

"Kind of," he replied. "I just graduated from the Atlantic School of Theology."

My face must have looked blank with lack of recognition, so he came to my rescue.

"It's a divinity college. They're affiliated with Saint Mary's University in Halifax."

"Ah," my eyes lit up. "I've been to Halifax several times. Silver and I used to walk by Saint Mary's on the way to Point Pleasant Park and the harbor!"

"Right. Having graduated, I was just ordained in the church, but haven't been assigned to a congregation yet. My dad surprised me by coming up to Halifax to help celebrate. He drove up from New York, took the ferry from Bangor, Maine, and showed up out of the blue. He insisted on taking me on a cross-country, father-and-son vacation as a kind of graduation present… To get back to your question, the clerical collar isn't required but I've been experimenting with wearing it when I'm trying to be 'on duty' and leaving it aside when I need a break and some personal time."

"How is it working out?"

"Actually, it's working out pretty well," his eyes lit up, and he flashed a brilliant smile. "With the collar on, people naturally assume I'm on duty, and they just assume that it's OK to come up and start a conversation with me. I thought that they'd first want to know what religion I follow, but for most people it doesn't seem to matter that much."

"Because they mostly just want someone to talk to?" I ventured.

"Exactly!" He gave me another big smile. "It's amazing how complete strangers will come and start a conversation when I'm wearing the collar. It seems to make it socially acceptable, even though I might be a complete stranger. It's like it gives them advance permission, and even a promise that I'll listen to them – which I will, of course."

"I imagine that it also gives you a chance to practice your religious knowledge," I added, looking meaningfully at the bible he had laid on the table between us.

"Not very often, actually. Most of the conversations aren't about religion at all, and I've even had some people tell me flat out that they're agnostics, or even atheists, but somehow they still hope to get a sympathetic ear."

"And you provide it?"

"Of course! It can be hard through. Some of the situations people find themselves in, or get themselves into, are heart-rending. After they leave, I sometimes feel like crawling off somewhere to take the collar off and have a good cry."

"I can image," I said. "I get that sometimes too."

"Of course you must, in your job too… I'm sorry, I should have realized that right off."

"It's OK," I replied. "I only meant that I understand what it's like." Then, sensing an opening, "But you must get the religious questions too. I couldn't help overhearing parts of a discussion about the meaning of biblical quotations with another young man in the dining car."

"Ah, with Ben. Yes. I'm sorry if it disturbed your meal. Ben is a very intense fellow, and he gets easily worked up. He's been challenging me with contradictions in the bible."

"Don't you mind? It must be a bit disconcerting to be challenged that way?"

"Not at all. I don't take it personally…" He paused as if thinking about what he'd just said. "OK, I mostly don't take it personally…" Another huge smile. "I enjoy the discussions, they're very good practise for me: they make me think and re-evaluate my own thoughts. Besides… it's become something of a competition."

"Really?"

"Yes. In fact, he ran out of challenges after our first few arguments, so now he's secretly reading the bible looking for new things to challenge me on!"

I had to smile at that. "So, you're actually making him read the bible?"

He just smiled back at me and knowingly placed an extended finger alongside his nose.

"Do you think he's likely to 'get religion' as they say?"

"Maybe not," he replied, with a shrug, "who knows? Sometimes the fiercest critics can become the most fervent converts. Anything is possible."

He paused in thought for a moment, then continued. "But, in Ben's case, I can't escape the feeling that there's something underneath it all that's grating on him. There's an anger there that he hasn't resolved, and I suspect it has nothing much to do with religion… or lack of religion even… In any case, I'm doing the little bit that I can." The latter thought was accompanied by another of his broad smiles.

I looked at him, with new eyes. "If you don't mind me saying so, I think you're going to be very good at your profession."

"I hope so," he said, but he sounded pleased. "You seem to be pretty good at yours too, if you don't mind me saying so. You've gotten me to go through this whole thing about getting people to open up and listening to them, while you've been doing it to me the whole time. And you've made me feel better too. I was sitting here feeling a bit melancholy until now."

"Thank you, and you're welcome," I replied doing my best to give him a bright smile in return.

That created a slightly awkward silence that was quickly broken by Cleo the cat, who suddenly decided that it was time to move along. Standing up and stretching, she very slowly walked across Nathan's lap, looking warily at Silver the whole time.

Just as she was preparing to jump into the aisle, I said "Silver," in warning. As the cat made her jump and trotted off, Silver, who had been watching Cleo closely, said "*Eerrrr,*" and looked up at me with his own version of a wide-eyed, innocent expression. It reminded me so much of Nathan's innocent expressions that I actually giggled.

I was saved from further embarrassment by Nathan's rising to his feet, and saying that he needed to go check on his father.

"It was nice meeting you," I said.

"You too!" He gave me another dazzling smile, and a friendly nod. "See you around."

I continued, for a while, to sit in the dome section, with Silver's head in my lap and watching the unending sequences of lakes and forests go by. As other passengers came and went, a few others struck up conversations when they sat across from us. In succession, I met a couple of university student friends travelling to take up summer jobs in tourist hotspots like Jasper and Banff, then a youngish tourist couple from Germany on their first visit to Canada, then late-middle-aged Newfoundland couple travelling with us as far as Edmonton. From there, they explained, they would be renting a car to drive north to Fort McMurray to visit their two sons, both of whom had moved there to get jobs in the booming oil sands industry.

I explained that, two years earlier, I had spent some time on assignment in Fort McMurray[6]. This information triggered a torrent of questions about the oil sands industry, Fort McMurray, and Alberta in general, and I was kept busy answering questions for at least an hour. They seemed like such a nice couple, that I found that I didn't mind in the least.

By this time, the dome section had completely filled up with passengers and, when there was a lull in the conversation, I decided it was a good time to release our seats so others could enjoy the unfolding panoramas so I said goodbye and wished them well with the rest of their trip.

Strolling forward along the train, we encountered Jack sitting alone in the coffee shop and joined him for a while, during which I related my earlier conversation with Nathan.

"It all sounds consistent with what we've already observed," judged Jack, when I was done. "It seems like all we have to do is stake you out somewhere beside an empty seat and people practically line up to talk to you." He seemed amused by the notion.

I decided to take him seriously this time. "In that case, maybe I'll try the other dome after lunch. I'd like to have a try at Ben."

The train hadn't stopped for quite a while that morning and, looking at our watches, we saw that the next stop would be in Sioux Lookout. If we arrived on schedule, we'd be there for half an hour, and decided that would be a good opportunity for a walk around the train - partly to be consistent with our role as observers of security details, but mostly to get some exercise and fresh air.

After Sioux Lookout, we had lunch, after which Silver and I took a stroll down the full length of the train, hoping for an opportunity to meet Ben in person. He was nowhere to be seen, however, so I gave up and found a double seat on upper deck of the Skyline Dome car. Watching the scenery, I was noticing that the many lakes and forests were becoming interspaced with broad expanses of bare rock – evidence of the Canadian Shield – when I heard a perky voice say "Hi." It was Hannah.

Smiling, I waved toward the facing seats, which had just been vacated, and said "Hi yourself." As she took a seat, Silver immediately abandoned me to go across and sit beside Hannah, where he contentedly allowed himself to be petted. Over the past few years, I'd found Silver's instincts to be uncannily perceptive. *If he thinks she's OK, then she probably is,* I thought.

Hannah didn't seem to be after anything more than someone to talk to, and it occurred to me that it might be that she wanted someone female to talk to. I tried testing this theory a bit. "How are you doing with the two boys?"

"You were right, I think they are trying to compete for me," she said, leaning forward conspiratorially. "It was fun at first, but it's become boring now." She sighed. "Nathan's really nice – almost too good to be true – you know?"

I nodded. I felt a bit that way myself. "And the other one?"

"Ben? He's interesting, and that sense of darkness he has about him was intriguing at first, but he has these flashes of anger that worry me sometimes." She bit her lip, thoughtfully.

"What's he doing on the train, do you know?"

"Oh. Yes. He's a university student, somewhere, and he's kind of like the rest of us - travelling across Canada to see the country. He says he plans to look for a job when we get to Vancouver."

We chatted further, while half watching the scenery go by, but I didn't really learn anything more. When our conversation tapered off, we both got up so others could take our places and watch the views, and we went our separate ways. As we did, I reflected that I'd learned a bit about Ben, but it didn't seem like I'd learned anything useful. *Oh well.*

As we continued west, toward Winnipeg, there were so many lakes and waterways that we crossed a seemingly endless number of bridges, which was always interesting. Some of railway stations in the towns along the way were right beside lakes, like the one at Minaki, Ontario, where we stopped for a couple of minutes to pick up some passengers.

We didn't go to the dining car that evening. Like many passengers, we had decided to wait for Winnipeg, which was one of the longer station-stops.

Although we arrived in Winnipeg a bit late, at 8 pm, we still had an hour and half before departing so most passengers took the opportunity to disembark and wander around the downtown area. Jack and Silver and I went off in search of a restaurant with an outdoor terrace, so Silver could sit with us. We were very close to the national historic site called The Forks, so we walked there and found several nice places to eat nearby. After a nice dinner, it was a short stroll to the shore of the Red River, and we had a nice walk along what, in later years, would be developed as The Forks Riverwalk.

Before heading back to the train, I found a pay-phone and tried calling my boss in Ottawa. He wasn't in and there were still no messages for me. *Oh well, the wheels turn slowly*, I thought. While I was at the phone, I also put in a call to my boyfriend Don to let him know where I was. We didn't exchange much real news, but it was good just to hear his voice.

The train departed on schedule at 9:30 pm, and I had just sat down in my roomette and was wondering what to do next when there was a knock on my door. It was François.

"There's been another break-in! Can you come?" He sounded affronted that such things should be happening on his train.

"What, again? The same room?"

"No! No, it was the Colonel's room this time, and it's a mess."

So, I got up and followed him down the corridor, with Silver trailing behind. The Colonel and Hannah were standing just outside the open door to their roomette. The Colonel looked angry, and Hannah looked pale and shocked. When everyone stood aside so I could peer in, I saw that François had spoken the literal truth: it was indeed a mess.

It was also a study on contrasts. The roomette had been made up while we were all off the train in Winnipeg, and the two berths had their sheets, blankets, and pillows neatly, even perfectly in place, even down to the little packages of chocolate bar on each pillow.

Their carry-on bags, and what I assumed was the Colonel's

briefcase, however, were lying open as if they had been simply cast aside, and clothes, books, and papers were scattered across the lower berth. Some had fallen, or been cast, onto the floor.

As I looked around, I could hear fragments of the Colonel giving François a piece of his mind, "...in all my years... how the railway can let this kind of thing happen... in this day and age... having paid your goddam exorbitant fares... the least you could have done..." and so on.

I tried to tune out the Colonel, look at everything, and think. No one could doubt that there'd been a break-in this time, and if Oliver Risk was who I thought he was, and given that I knew exactly who the Colonel was, there was no way that this was some random intrusion. *But why be so obvious this time?* I wondered. *To send a message? Or because the intruder was in a great hurry?* I suspected the latter.

As I considered, the sounds of the Colonel berating François broke into my thoughts, to be quickly interrupted by the sound of Jack's voice asking what was the matter.

"Ah, Constable, I'm so glad you're here!" François had leapt at Jack's arrival like it was a life-buoy, and gave him a quick summary of what had happened.

I moved out of the way so Jack could squeeze in and take a look. While he did that, I stepped over to Hannah and asked if she was feeling OK.

"Oh, yes, I'm fine. It's just the shock, you know? You read about things like this in detective stories but you never expect them to happen to you. Do you?"

"Well, you hope not, that's for sure... Can I ask you and your dad a few questions?"

"I'll answer any questions you have," said the Colonel, who had overheard and was either feeling protective of Hannah, or else in need of asserting some control over the situation.

I decided to play along. "Thank you, Sir," and fed him a short-list of initial questions:

"Who discovered the break-in?"	The Colonel and Hannah.
"When?"	When they boarded the train.
"Was anything damaged?"	No.
"Is anything missing?"	No.
"Did they see or hear anyone?"	No.

Meanwhile, Jack had come out of the roomette and gave me a questioning look. I shook my head to indicate that I hadn't learned anything useful from the Peters.

We had just asked them to tell François, or one of us, if they discovered or remembered anything new, and were about to leave when I thought of one more question. "Is there anything in your room that shouldn't be there?"

"No," said the Colonel, more as an instinctive reaction than anything I thought, but Hannah had a puzzled look on her face and went back into the roomette and looked around again.

She was back almost immediately carrying a tie. "I didn't really think of it until you asked, but this doesn't belong here."

It was a clip-on tie. The kind with a permanently tied knot that can be quickly clipped or unclipped from a dress shirt with all the buttons done up.

The tie was in VIA Rail colours.

François was outraged and, before the Colonel could start in on him again, he was full of indignation, with promises of swift investigation, and dark insinuations about punishment for the guilty party, whomever that might be. He promised to immediately interview all of the train's staff in an effort to uncover the culprit.

It was his train and we still didn't have much of a crime on our hands so we left him to it. Before taking our leave, however, I asked if I could hold onto the tie for a while and went back to my roomette to get a plastic bag in which to preserve it.

It was after 11pm, and the train had just made a brief stop at Portage la Prairie, when François found Jack and I sitting at a table having a cup of late-night coffee. He was still visibly upset.

"Nothing! Not a damn thing eh?" he pronounced, as he sat down with us.

"I take it that no one broke down and confessed?" asked Jack.

"Everyone denies everything. No one saw or heard anything," he sighed. "Now that I've had time to think about it, I can't believe it was one of the crew." Seeing our expressions, he hurried on: "It's not stubborn loyalty. The railroad's like a family, eh? We've worked together a long time… we look after each other… there's no reason to do something like this."

"Well, for what it's worth, I don't think it's member of the crew either," I offered.

"You don't?"

"No. I think it's the same person that searched the Risks' roomette last night. Whomever it is, I think they're looking for something specific."

"Specific? Like what?"

"I don't know for sure. Something small. Maybe some kind of documents, since even the file folders in briefcases have been rifled."

"What about the tie then?"

"Remember how last night's villain was disguised as a nun? Well I suspect that tonight's villain was disguised as a VIA Rail attendant. There was a crew change in Winnipeg, right? So, if a VIA Rail employee on the train saw another employee that they didn't recognize, wouldn't they just assume that it was someone from the other crew?"

"Probably, yes... no, I'm sure they would, because the crew that left are based in Toronto and they'll be working back on an eastbound train. They would all know each other, but not necessarily the crew that is based in Winnipeg. Whew, I feel much better now, eh?"

I found it interesting that François was more worried about the possibility of a crew member going bad than he was about the break-ins themselves, but I supposed that it was only natural. When François left, we were alone in the dining area. In a low voice, I asked Jack what he thought about it all.

"Well, if the break-ins aren't a coincidence, then I think you're right about them being the work of one person, using different disguises. I also think that if our mystery person hasn't found what they're looking for then they'll try again. Not getting caught either time will have boosted their confidence too. Where do you think they'll strike next?"

"I think the baggage car might be a target. Other than that, the only connection I've noted so far is through the three young people. Maybe Ben's roomette will be the next target, or maybe Ben is our mystery person."

"You don't like him, do you?"

That startled me. "No, I don't, but I'm trying to keep an open mind... Is it that obvious?"

"No, I don't think so. It's just that I know you pretty well now and I can sense that his attitude grates on you."

"Well, it does, but thanks for pointing it out. I'll try to keep my thoughts from showing… If you were going to try the baggage car, when would you make your attempt?"

Jack paused in thought for a moment, then brought out his copy of the railway timetable. "Once we cross into Saskatchewan, the main stops are in Melville, Saskatoon, and Biggar. We're scheduled to leave Biggar at 1:40 pm. After that, we'll only stop for advance requests until tomorrow night when we reach Edmonton at 8:50. The best odds of breaking into the baggage car without being caught should be between Biggar and Edmonton. That's how I'd do it."

"I agree," I said. "Want to take turns watching the baggage car?"

"You're a bit too noticeable. How about if I do it. I'll dress in plain clothes and ask François if I can borrow some kind of worker's jacket and maybe a hat or toque, and then I'll plant myself in the café part of the Skyline Dome car where I'll have a clear view of the door to the baggage car."

I agreed to this, and we walked back to our roomettes together.

That night, I was sitting up in bed, with Silver curled up beside me, watching the stars in the sky and the occasional light of civilization flash by, wondering what the next day would be like. Between the connections that were forming between some of the people I was watching and the sequence of break-ins, I was starting to feel the anticipation that comes when you shift from data gathering to hunting, and I remember thinking that the next day would probably be interesting.

I had no idea.

Laurie Schramm

6 THE PRAIRIES

Day 5
May 30, 1978
Crossing into Saskatchewan

I'd slept well, having come to appreciate the gentle rolling of the train and having gotten used to the dim thudding of the wheels on the tracks below. The day began quietly enough. Once again, there were only a few early-birds in the dining car for breakfast. I had a leisurely meal while enjoying the change in scenery. Heading west from Winnipeg, we progressively left behind most of the forests and lakes in favour of the prairies. While some people thought of the prairies as 'flat and boring,' I always found it interesting with the huge skies and the unending patchwork of fields, towns, and rivers. Later in the summer it would be even better: when the different crops began to bloom there would be brilliant, contrasting colours. Like fields of golden yellow canola next to fields of soft blue flax. The peaceful looking, wide-open spaces put me in a reflective mood that was only broken by brief visits from Jack and François.

There was a scheduled one-hour stop at Saskatoon just before lunchtime, and Silver and I got off to do one of our routine walks around the whole train, take a few notes, and make a call to my boss in Ottawa. I actually got him on the line this time. He didn't have any solid information on Benjamin (Ben) Shaw yet, but when I briefly described the patterns Jack and I had observed he offered a couple of thoughts on the kind of person that might be watching the

Risks and Peters families. His thoughts were interesting, but didn't really change anything. I left him with one more request: would he please have someone check all of the car rental agencies in Edson, Hinton, and Jasper for any reservations booked for the next few days in the names of Risk, Peters, or Shaw. I said that I expected to be able to call from Edmonton when we arrived at about 11 pm that evening. I also made a few other requests while I was at it.

Once we had re-boarded it was lunchtime, so Silver and I went and took our accustomed table in the dining car. This time the young people were seated at the table right beside us. Hannah flashed us a smile and a wave when she came in, and I was about to initiate a conversation with her when the two young men arrived.

As they came in, they were arguing – again.

"We only have to look out for our own sins," Nathan was saying. "That's how we will be judged. The Bible says: *'Fathers shall not be put to death for their children, nor children put to death for their fathers; each is to die for his own sin,'* Deuteronomy 24:16. And both Jeremiah and Ezekiel talk about how people will only die for their own sins."

Ben pounced on this with unusual heat, however. "Ah ha! But the Bible clearly says that children have to be punished for their parents' sins. How about the book of Exodus where it talks about God punishing the children for the sins of the parents?"

Nathan took a breath in preparation to answer this, but he didn't get a chance as Ben rushed on. "And Jeremiah talks about God taking vengeance on people because their ancestors forsook him. Right?" Ben's tone and body language suggested that this particular argument was more than academic, and more than competition for a girl's attention.

This is what Ben has been leading up to all along with these arguments, I thought.

Ben seemed to win this round, too, as Nathan merely replied "I don't know what to tell you Ben. I think it's the difference between things God has done himself, and the things he wants us to do. Like when chain-smoking parents tell their kids not to smoke. Sort of 'Do what I say, not what I do.' You know?"

"Yes, I know all right!" said Ben, sounding angry as he got up again and marched out of the car.

Nathan gave a huge sigh. "I don't think I'm helping him."

At this, Hannah actually unbent a little and placed a consoling hand on his shoulder. "All you can do is try Nathan." She seemed to be looking at him with new eyes. "You really do care, don't you?"

"Of course I do, but I don't seem to be able to find the right words to help him."

"I think you may be helping him more than you know," she replied, thoughtfully. "I don't think this is about religion or faith at all. I think he's trying to work through some kind of personal issues, and I think you're helping him by just giving him a way to talk things out."

"That's a kind thought, Hannah. Thank you."

I thought Hanna was probably right. With Ben having stormed off Nathan and Hanna settled into a friendly discussion of some kind that I couldn't clearly overhear, and then they were joined by the Colonel who didn't seem to be as disapproving of Nathan as he clearly was of Ben. Their three-way conversation must have turned religious at some point, as Nathan opened up his bible to look up some kind of quote or passage.

After lunch, the views leading west of Saskatoon continued to be mostly farms on slowly undulating terrain, with the occasional river and town. There was a short stop at the town of Biggar, and then we continued making our way across the rest of the prairies to Alberta.

At this point I was curious to see what Jack's stakeout looked like, so Silver and I walked the length of the train as far as the baggage car. When we turned back, at the front end of the Skyline Dome car, we were in the coffee shop and there at the furthest table from the front of the car was what appeared to be an engineer or mechanic-type railway worker of some kind. As we walked by his table, I looked at him out of the corners of my eyes and saw what I was supposed to see: a tired-looking fellow wearing a grease-stained beige-leather jacket and one of those black-and-white-striped engineer's caps, and huddled over his coffee cup as if it was the most important thing in the world.

I didn't want to draw any attention to Jack, or even appear to recognize him, so I kept my body and head pointed straight ahead and walked the rest of the way through the car. It was hard to keep a straight face, but I managed.

After lunch, Silver and I took a casual stroll along the rest of the train. There was no sign of Oliver Risk or the Colonel, but I spotted Ben in the bar, alone and drinking. At the rear of the train, I noticed Nathan and Hannah sitting together in the upper section of the Park Dome Car. The rest of the upper section was full, as usual, so Silver and I just continued on and tried our luck with the upper section of the Skyline Dome Car. I was glad I did, because a pair of seats had opened up at the very front of the dome, facing forward.

We now had two of the very best viewing seats on the train and we spend the next two hours with a panoramic view of the approaching scenery. The best view came just west of Wainwright, Alberta, as we approached and then crossed the Fabyan Trestle Bridge. This is a turn-of-the-century style bridge that crossed a broad, shallow valley with Battle River at the bottom. Opened in 1909, it was only about 60 m high but it was nearly a kilometer long! From my vantage point high up on the train, it looked like a long curtain of rust-coloured iron, with what must have been at least fifty double sets of pylons individually anchored in concrete footings. When I mentioned it to François later, he told me that when it was built, it was the largest railway structure in Canada.

Although I always went for the first seating at dinner, this time everyone else seemed to have the same idea as the dining car almost immediately filled, nearly to capacity. Partly for that reason, it was noisy too, so I had no hope of overhearing any interesting conversations. I did notice Oliver and Nathan Risk enter and get seated by themselves, soon followed by Hannah, who joined them. I noticed with some amusement that Ben was seated well past Hannah and the Risks, and facing away from them. *He won't be watching them at dinner this time*, I thought. I didn't spot the Colonel, and assumed that he either ate later or in the coffee shop, if at all.

From 5:30 pm onwards there were no more stops until we reached Edmonton at around 10 pm. The train had no sooner come to a halt in the station than Jack stopped at my open door with a bundle under his arm. I could see that it was the engineer/mechanic-type jacket he'd been wearing all afternoon.

"Any luck?" I asked.

He grimaced. "Nothing but a painfully full bladder. I only had one cup of coffee the whole time but it was more than I had room for."

I smiled, trying hard not to laugh out loud. "We've got three hours in the station here, how about coming for a walk?"

"Sure, let me give the jacket and hat back to François and I'll meet you on the platform."

While we waited for Jack, Silver and I walked along the outside of the train, watched the baggage handlers load and unload bags from the baggage car, then back. When he joined us, we wandered around the station for a while, then went in search of a payphone.

When I called my boss' number I didn't expect him to be in the office but I hoped the duty officer would have a message for me. He did.

"Got your notebook handy?" he asked, "it's a long one."

I told him when I was ready, and the next few minutes were spent writing as he read the message to me. Jack was standing beside me, watching to make sure I wouldn't be overheard, so he got to hear the whole message as I read it back to the duty officer. When he confirmed that I had it all, I thanked him and hung up.

"Well, no messages for me for days and now it all comes at once. We now know who Ben is, and we already knew about the Colonel…"

"And there's no doubt now about who Oliver Risk is," supplied Jack.

"I guess not," I added. "We'll have to have a chat with François in the morning."

Laurie Schramm

7 ALBERTA

Day 6
May 31, 1978

It was midnight when the train pulled out of Edmonton, and it felt like I'd just gotten to sleep when I awoke to knocking on my door. It was François.

"I thought you should know. Someone's broken into the baggage car, eh? Everything looks OK, but I thought you'd like to know."

"OK, have you told Jack?"

"Yes. He's getting dressed."

"Give me a moment and we'll come too."

It was only when I was dressing that I realized that the train wasn't moving. A look out the window confirmed that we were stopped at a small town somewhere. It was 1:30 am.

It was only a few minutes before we were all ready, and François led us to the baggage car. There were scratches and large dents on both the doorframe, near the lock, and the aluminum-clad door itself. It looked like the door had been forced with something like a crowbar.

"One of the attendants noticed when we stopped here in Evansburg to pick up a passenger, eh? He came and got me, and we took a look around but it doesn't look like anything is missing. Who breaks into a place and doesn't take anything?"

"Maybe they were interrupted before they could do anything more," I said, but that wasn't my first thought. As we stood there, looking at the luggage sitting in the racks I happened to make eye contact with Jack. We were both thinking the same thing.

"Could you help us find the bags belonging to the Risks please?"

That brought a shrewd gleam into François' eyes. "I had a feeling you were on the train to do more than just assess security. That kind of thing has been done many times before, and not much changes on the railroads, eh?"

"I'm sorry François. We weren't able to tell you everything unless there was an emergency."

"That's OK," he said, "it's made things interesting, with the missing nun and the phantom attendant. Something to tell the grandchildren one day."

As he was speaking, he led the way to the racks of luggage that were destined for Vancouver, and the three of us set about pulling the bags out and checking the name tags. We found two bags bearing tags marked for Oliver and Nathan. It was an anticlimax, though, as they seemed to be perfectly intact. Although each bag was locked with a small padlock, the locks were intact and showed no signs of tampering.

"Huh," said Jack, sitting back on his heels after inspecting the locks. "These little locks are the easiest things to the world to open. Nothing like the work that went into prying the car door open. Either our intruder had the keys or they didn't get as far as the bags."

"Maybe they were after something else," I said. "Let's see if we can find the Peters' bags."

"I saw them when we were looking for these ones," said Jack. "Hang on a moment."

It only took a couple of minutes for him to work backwards and find the Peters' bags. Again, there were two. At first sight, they too seemed undisturbed... except that neither of them had locks securing the wrap-around zippers that sealed the bags shut.

"Either they're very trusting people, or the locks have been removed. Do you have a flashlight I can borrow?" I asked François.

"But of course." He went to the end of the car, where there was a heavy-duty-looking flashlight secured in spring-clips beside the door to the generator-boiler car. Bringing it back, he handed it to me.

With the aid of the flashlight, I tried looking in the corners, nooks, and crannies of the car, not finding anything helpful until I tried looking at the racks we'd just cleared of their luggage. There, lying on the floor near the wall were two broken locks.

"Our intruder seems to have wanted a look at the Peters' luggage," I said, pocketing the locks. "Let's take a look."

Placing them on the floor, Jack and I each opened one up. Both appeared to be full, but the contents were in disarray, as if they'd been taken out and then simply stuffed back in.

"Well, either the Risks are both messy packers or these have been searched," said Jack.

"Yes, and look here," The inside lining of the top of the Colonel's bag came away when I touched it. "The lining has been slit open with a knife."

"Same with this one," said Jack, "prodding gently at the lining of Hannah's. I think our intruder has been looking for documents."

"Yes," I agreed… *Or a map,* I thought. "François, would you be willing to help us with a little deception?"

"What do you have in mind?" he asked.

"Would you be willing to pretend that all you found was the broken door, you came and got us, and we all looked together but there was no other apparent damage, and it didn't look like anything was stolen tonight?"

"But that is exactly what has happened. Where is the pretend?"

"I'd like for us to put all these bags back into the racks, and pretend that we didn't notice that these two bags have no locks."

A smile crept into onto François' face. "And those two little locks you found could have belonged to anyone, heh? Could have been lying there for months for all anyone knows."

"Exactly, and if the Peters come to you in the morning complaining that their luggage has been disturbed?"

"I will be my usual helpful self, eh? We will inspect the luggage together. I will be very shocked and conciliatory, and we will do lots of paperwork, of course!"

"Actually, I doubt they'll even come and talk to you about it. So you might not have to pretend anything, OK?"

"*D'accord,* as long as you come back one day and tell me what it was all about, OK?"

Jack and I nodded our agreement.

"One more request?" I asked of François.

He looked at me expectantly.

"If anyone asks you to let them off at one of the next stops, just do everything as you would normally do it and then tell us about it at breakfast. We'll be in the dining car early; about 5:30."

He raised his eyebrows, as if to ask questions, then thought better of it, nodded, and simply said, "Let's clean up then, eh?"

I didn't feel able to tell him that I'd received a message informing me that, while none of our people of interest had booked rental vehicles in Edson, there was one booking in Hinton, and another one in Jasper.

We put all the luggage back into place and left, with François pulling the damaged car door closed as best he could.

***

When the train pulled into the small station at Edson, Alberta, it was 3:10 am, only slightly behind schedule. Only one passenger disembarked at the station, then waited for a few minutes while his checked luggage was retrieved. Only a few blocks away, the Yellowhead Highway had split into separate one-way sections as it crossed through the town. In between the two lanes were a variety of services, conveniently placed so that drivers going in either direction could pull over for food, gas, or shopping. Among the amenities were a cluster of medium-sized motels. It was toward these that Ben walked, backpack on his back, and his carry-on and checked bags in each hand.

At this time of night, there was only the occasional semi-trailer truck or other vehicle travelling the highway.

Within four blocks he was standing where he had a good view of four motels. Choosing the nearest motel, he walked into the lobby, which was empty. Looking around, he found the small alcove, close to the elevators, where several luggage carts sat empty – waiting for the next guests to arrive or depart.

Selecting a cart, he placed his backpack and bags on it and wheeled it into the corridor. The large rubber-shod wheels were silent as he pushed the cart down the corridor, following the Fire Exit signs to find the back door leading to the rear parking lot.

Stooping to remove a long, thin piece of metal from his backpack, he left everything else on the cart, by the door. Then, he picked up the door stop that lay just inside the door and put it in his pocket. Finally, carefully testing first to made sure that it did not lock behind him, he went outside and crossed the parking lot, heading for the other motels.

Not liking the looks of the first motel he came to, which had outfitted its parking lot with an array of high-intensity lights, he passed it by. He also walked past the next motel for the same reason. The next motel however, had lighting in its parking lot but there were a few corners, at the extreme ends of its lot, that were not well lit. He headed for one of those.

Now to choose a car. He was looking for a car with manual door locks, but more than that, he was looking for something common. He knew that the most popular passenger car sold in 1977 and 1978 was the Chevrolet Impala, or its upscale model, the Chevrolet Caprice. The most common vehicle colours of the 1970s were green, beige, yellow, or gold.

Wouldn't you know it, he thought to himself, no Impalas in sight.

There was, however, a mud-covered beige Ford F100 half-ton truck sitting there. Pickup trucks, he knew, were as common in Alberta as cars were in Ontario. Oh well, when in Alberta…, he thought.

Taking a quick look around, to make sure no one seemed to be watching, he took out two tools. The wooden doorstop that he'd stolen from the motel he pushed in-between the driver-side door and roof to create a slight opening. Into this he inserted the long, thin piece of metal he'd retrieved from his backpack. This was a 'Slim Jim,' a thin piece of metal nearly two feet long with a hook shape cut into one end. It was the kind of tool a tow-truck would carry for helping motorists that have locked their keys inside their vehicle. By its very nature, it was also the kind of tool thieves could use to enter a locked vehicle.

Working the hooked end down and over towards the locking knob near the bottom of the window, he maneuvered the tool back and forth, trying to get the hook to catch the flared top of locking knob. It took half a dozen tries before he finally caught to top of the knob with the hook. Then, with a careful upwards pull, the knob came up, and the door was unlocked.

Withdrawing the Slim Jim, he opened the door, at which point the doorstop fell to the ground. He kicked it under the truck. Entering the truck, he carefully shut the door so the dome light would turn off, and slid across the bench seat to the passenger side.

Reaching into his jacket, he then removed his next two tools: a Swiss-Army-style pocketknife and a small flashlight. Twisting so he was lying with his torso underneath the steering column, with his head facing up, he turned his flashlight on and held it between his teeth. Thus armed, he *navigated through the various coils of wire until he'd located the three main bundles of wires: two leading to controls like signal lights and windshield wipers, and a third that connected the ignition switch to the battery and starter that lie on the other side of the engine firewall. Pulling aside this latter bundle, he looked at the wire colours.*

One of the wires he identified as bringing power directly from the battery system. Using his knife, he cut it and stripped some of the plastic insulation back from the end of the segment that led from the firewall. Another of the wires he identified as the one that normally received power with the ignition key in the 'On' position. This he cut, exposed the metal on one end, and connected to one of the red wires. The dashboard lights and radio immediately turned on. So far, so good, *he thought, reaching to switch off the radio.*

Next, he identified the starter wire that normally received power with the ignition key in the 'Start' position. This he cut, then exposed the metal on the end leading to the engine compartment. Holding this wire carefully, he touched it momentarily to the battery wire. The engine started. Reaching over to the floor pedals, he pushed the gas pedal once to rev the engine — to make sure it didn't stall — then tucked the bare wire out of the way and levered himself out from under the steering column.

Now the engine was running but the steering wheel was still locked. With the screwdriver blade of his knife he pried off the metal keyhole plate, then jiggled the blade around inside the lock cylinder until the lock-spring came free.

With this, he was able to ease the truck out of the lot, drive back to the first motel to pick up his backpack and bags, and he was ready to go.

It was 4 am. With luck, it would be at least another two hours before the theft of the truck was noticed, maybe more. He estimated that it would take almost an hour to drive to Hinton. Another hour's driving after that should put him in Jasper by 6 am.

The train was scheduled to arrive in Jasper at 6:30.

Plenty of time, *Ben thought.*

***

The train's next stop was at the town of Hinton; arriving at 4 am. This time, two passengers disembarked and collected their luggage.

Like Edson, the town had many of its businesses located along the length of the highway. Unlike Edson, however, the highway did not split into one-way lanes, and there was no particular cluster of services. As a result, the services stretched along the full length of the portion of the highway that ran through the town.

Using a pay phone to call for a taxi, they sat down to wait as the train pulled out of the station, heading for the Rocky Mountains. Its next stop would be Jasper.

When the taxi arrived, they asked it to take them to the nearest place they could eat, which turned out to be a 24-hour truck-stop at the edge of town. They took their time over breakfast, because the automotive dealership from which they had booked a rental car didn't open until 8 am.

Unfortunately, the car rental company was at the easternmost edge of town, nearly a mile away. Not wanting to carry their luggage that far, at 7:30 they used the truck-stop's pay phone to call for another taxi to take them to the dealership. They were sitting with their luggage outside the door of the dealership when the service manager arrived to open up at 7:45, and the manager took pity on them and let them in right away. As a result, by 8 am they had completed the paperwork, and were stowing their luggage in a two-tone eggshell-white and brown Dodge Aspen.

It would take about an hour to drive to Jasper, which should have them there by 9 am.

As they pulled onto the highway and out of town, heading for Jasper National Park, Hannah Peters resumed her conversation with the Colonel: trying to understand why he had been so determined to get off the train early and make the trip through the mountains by car instead.

They didn't notice the mud-covered, beige pickup truck that was about half a mile behind them.

***

Having had only two-and-a-half hours' sleep, it was a struggle to get up and get to the dining car, and I arrived feeling grumpy and desperate for coffee. I didn't have the Hollywood-stereotypical cop's love for doughnuts, but countless long shifts, and especially long night-shifts, had addicted me to strong, black coffee. On the flip side, once Silver and I were seated in the dining car and I'd had my first half-cup, I was starting to feel human again. This was fortunate, because it was then that Jack joined us, followed in short order by François.

François' expression showed plainly that he had news for us.

"How did you sleep, eh?"

"Hardly at all," I said, still a bit grumpily.

"Great," said Jack, brightly. Looking at his face, I could see that it was true. He looked as bright-eyed and bushy-tailed as ever, making me feel uncharitably jealous.

I couldn't fool Jack though. Once glance at me told him what I was thinking, and he tried to soften the blow. "Don't worry, it always hits me on the second day. Tomorrow morning I'll feel like hell."

"Promise?" I asked, feeling just a little bit better.

Our morning banter was cut short at this point by François, who couldn't contain his news any longer.

"We had one passenger make us stop in Edson so he could get off!"

"It was Ben Shaw, right?"

François' jaw dropped. "How did you know?"

"Just a lucky guess. I'll tell you why in a moment. Did anyone get off in Hinton?"

"Suddenly, I have the feeling you know that one too," said François, but he answered anyway. "It was the Colonel and his daughter."

"And they all took their luggage with them?"

"Yes, but that's not unusual. Passengers can get off wherever they like, and then re-book themselves to continue on a later train… Of course, they don't usually interrupt their trips at small towns like these, it's usually at big centres like Edmonton, or tourist spots like Jasper."

"OK, here's the thing. I think the Peters are following someone, and I think Ben is doing the same thing."

"Ah, *je comprends*. And neither party wants the other to know what they are up to, eh?"

"Right."

"And let me guess who it is that they're following…"

"Don't say it out loud." I interrupted. "But, I know what you're thinking, and yes that's who they're following."

"And you are following them too?"

"Yes. Don't ask why just yet. If you-know-who gets off in Jasper, then we will be doing the same. If that happens, can you arrange for us to be able to get off the other side of the train from the other passengers."

"So nobody sees you, right? It's no problem. Just come to the baggage car. I'll meet you at the broken door. If you want to get off, we'll get your bags and I'll let you out on the side away from the station, and I'll have one of the attendants help you carry your bags. If you walk forward, none of the passengers will be able to see you when you cross in front of the engine."

"That would be great, thank you François."

He chuckled. "Like I said, a story for the grandchildren, eh?"

"Would you like to be in one more thing?" I asked.

"*Bien sûr!*"

I noticed that bits of his mother-tongue slipped into conversation when he was excited. "Give us a few minutes to eat and then you can watch Silver do his stuff, OK?"

"OK."

Twenty minutes later, we'd eaten breakfast, François was back with us, and we all went to my roomette. Taking the VIA Rail tie from the plastic bag I'd stored it in, I showed it to Silver and let him give it a good sniff. Then, I asked him to track, and stood back.

Silver first went forward along the car's corridor, sniffing along the floor and back and forth from side to side, including at the various compartment doors. As he neared the forward end of the car, he sniffed around in the communal shower area, along the berth sections, and inside each of the two shared bathrooms. When he reached the door at the end of the car he stopped and looked at me.

"Let's try the other way," I said, and motioned for Silver to search in the other direction. This time, he walked slowly along the corridor until he neared our roomette, at which point he slowed down and went back to his thorough tracking routine.

He went like this for less than twenty feet before he stopped by one of the roomette doors, gave the door jam and sill a more thorough investigation, and then promptly sat down on his haunches and gave me his '*Found it!*' gaze.

"That is the roomette of Benjamin Shaw," exclaimed François.

"Yes. Let's try one more experiment, shall we?"

Retracing our steps, I went back to my roomette and exchanged the VIA tie for the rescued nun's habit. Once again, I let Silver have a really good sniff of it, then asked him to track the scent.

I didn't specify a direction to search this time, and Silver looked up at me for confirmation and then headed off on his own. There was no careful sniffing around everywhere this time, however, as he promptly walked straight to Ben's roomette and sat down.

As I was congratulating Silver and rewarding him with a few dog treats, François was still busy being amazed.

"He must have been the one that broke into the Risks' roomette and also the Peters'!"

"Yes, and almost certainly the baggage car as well," added Jack.

We asked if we could look inside the roomette, and François motioned his assent.

With the roomette being empty, the door wasn't locked, so I pushed it open. The lower berth was a mess of rumpled sheets, blankets, and towels.

"It hasn't been cleaned yet, eh?" said François.

"That's perfect for us," I replied, looking around more carefully this time. There wasn't anything hidden in the covers or under the mattress of the lower berth, nor for the upper berth. The small waste basket, however, was full. Spreading out the blankets on the lower berth, I dumped the waste basket contents on top and spread them out.

Apart from the gross stuff: soiled Kleenexes and mostly empty junk food wrappers, there was a wad of letter-size papers that had been rolled up and stuffed into the basket. That looked promising.

Clearing some space, I rolled out the papers. There were six of them, each of them bearing newspaper clippings that had been glued into place, with hand-written notations on the dates and names of the newspapers from which the clippings had come.

I looked up at Jack, who was standing beside me, and we exchanged a look and a nod.

"Here François, you may as well see what we've found but don't touch them, OK?"

As Jack made room, François came forward into the roomette and looked with interest at the newspaper headings. "Don't read them out loud," I cautioned.

When he looked up, wide-eyed, I touched my index finger to my lips and added, "Remember, don't ask us anymore and don't say anything to anyone – not for a day or two anyway, after that it won't matter."

"So you'll be getting off at Jasper," he asked, his eyes still wide.

I looked at my watch. It was 8:30, the train was running two hours late. We'd be stopping in Jasper very soon. "We'll meet you at the baggage car in a few minutes. We'll be able to tell you then."

As François hustled off to prepare for the next stop, I carefully gathered up the pages, handling them by the edges as much as I could, to avoid covering them with my fingerprints. I still had the nun's habit with me, so I used it to hold the papers and went back to my roomette to store them in bags and repack my carry-on bags. Jack went to do the same.

When we all met again at the baggage car door, François raised his eyebrows and said: "Mr. Risk and his son, the minister, told me they've suddenly decided to get off here and explore the mountains for a few days. We're just searching for their bags now. I suppose that means you're wanting to get off as well?"

I nodded. "Yes. Could you do one last thing and delay finding the Risks bags for ten minutes?"

Nodding his head, he slyly placed an extended index finger alongside his nose. He was enjoying his role in our intrigue.

"Thank you for all your help, and I won't forget to phone you later and tell you what it was all about – for your grandchildren!" I barely caught myself from adding "eh?," as I was afraid he might be insulted, but I couldn't help smiling to myself. François had been a helpful and enjoyable travel companion of sorts.

With the help of one of the attendants, who had appeared with a kind of wheelbarrow-for-luggage that had a huge front wheel, we got our checked bags and made our way around the far side of the train from the station platform and crossed in front of the locomotive. The attendant had no trouble pushing the wheelbarrow, with its large front wheel, over the rails and soon we were out of anyone's sight, skirting the far side of the train station.

When we reached the front corner of the station, the engine started in a nondescript-looking station wagon that had been waiting in the parking lot. It drove directly to us, and when the driver's window was rolled down, it revealed a uniformed RCMP Constable.

The constable identified himself, and got out to open the back of the station wagon for our luggage.

When we were all in pace in the car, he said that the Detachment was on the far side of town, and that they had everything ready that we'd asked for.

Now it's going to get interesting, I thought.

Photo courtesy of VIA Rail Canada (Resource ID 386).

8 RED PASS

Just before approaching the town of Jasper, we had been treated to a gorgeous sunrise that spread a pink hue over the east-facing slopes of the mountains. At 9 am, it was fully daylight as Jack and Silver and I parked a block away from the car rental company that my boss, Bob's team had discovered held a reservation for a Mr. James Peters, also known as the Colonel.

For our part, we were sitting in the same station wagon that had been used to pick us up from the train station, which turned out to be an unmarked police car. There were two more constables in a marked, highway patrol car, on standby too, but they were well out of sight, having positioned themselves at the outskirts of town – on the southwest side, where the Yellowhead Highway intersects the Columbia Icefields Parkway. We would stay in touch with them by radio.

Our position was on a connecting street, close to the junction, so that from my position in the passenger seat I had a clear view across to the street to the rental agency and its car lot.

We also knew the kind of vehicle that had been reserved – a full-size car - but not the exact make, model, or colour. I hoped to learn those details by watching through binoculars.

We only had to wait about ten minutes before Oliver and Nathan Risk showed up by taxi. As they got out, I was surprised to see that they had quite a few bags with them. In addition to their carry-on bags and Oliver Risk's briefcase, were three larger bags and a good-sized backpack.

After a few minutes in the agency, they emerged and made their way to the car lot. As they loaded their bags and then pulled away, I had binoculars in one hand and the police radio microphone in the other so I could relay descriptions. These would be noted by the highway patrol car outside of town and also the radio room operator in the Jasper Detachment.

"Persons of interest numbers one and two, Oliver Risk and Nathan Risk, driving a late-model Chev Caprice, two-tone light blue with white trim, Alberta licence number…"

Almost immediately, a car that had been parked about a block away, and on the same side of the road as the car rental agency, pulled away from the curb. It was driving in the same direction as the Risks. As the car passed us, I could see the Colonel and Hannah in the front seat, and radioed this in as well.

"Persons of interest numbers three and four, James Peters and Hannah Peters, driving a late-model Dodge Aspen, two-tone white or beige with brown trim, Alberta licence number…"

"Look there," said Jack, pointing further down the block.

There, about another block behind the spot where the Peters had been parked, a pickup truck had pulled away from the curve and was driving in the same direction as the Peters and the Risks.

I whistled as the truck approached and then passed us. It was Ben Shaw.

"This is like watching a scene from a TV or movie drama," I said to Jack, then went back to my radio reporting.

"Person of interest number five, Benjamin Shaw, driving a late-model Ford pickup truck, possibly beige in colour but covered in mud. Licence plate obscured by mud. Pickup truck is suspected to be stolen, possibly in Edson."

My last sight through the binoculars was of all three vehicles heading southwest on the main street, which the street signs all informed them would lead to the Yellowhead Highway once they were out of town. Since we thought we knew where they were going, we didn't bother trying to follow them. The highway patrol car would already be in motion to a predetermined location, near what we thought would be the second-most-likely place for the Risks to be heading.

Our plan was for Jack, Silver, and I to now drive directly to what we thought would be the first-most-likely place for the Risks to be heading, which was deep into the mountains, some 71 km (44 miles) away.

Jack is a more aggressive driver than I am, which is what we needed right now. He had already started the car and we pulled out, keeping well behind Ben. After only two blocks Jack took a hard, left-hand turn and accelerated as I switched on the small, magnetic-base, red-light flasher that was sitting in the front dash, nestled up against the front window. I didn't throw the flashing light outside and up onto the roof, because we only wanted vehicles that were directly in front of us to see it. Whereas the convoy of vehicles ahead of us had remained on the main street/highway, we were now on Hazel Avenue, going southeast, but only for two more blocks at which point we turned right onto the Yellowhead Highway. Here, the highway was clear, and the engine roared as Jack opened it up full throttle.

With us now travelling at least twice the speed of the others, we expected to reach the main highway junction ahead of them even though it was only about a kilometer ahead. I had my binoculars out again, watching for the upcoming cross-road.

"There they are," I said, as we approached the junction. "The Risks are about two blocks away."

Jack didn't slow down, as we had the right-of-way through the intersection. By the time the Risks reached the stop sign, then made their right-hand turn to follow, we were well ahead of them and still moving fast.

Although it was hardly a time for sight-seeing, we were now travelling through some of the most beautiful scenery in Canada. First, we passed the road to the Jasper Sky Tram, with the partially-snow-clad summit of Whistler Mountain visible above and behind it. Another 25 km (15 miles) brought us to the British Columbia border, and about the same distance again brought us into Mount Robson Provincial Park.

That it was a very clear day was obvious from the fact that we had an unusually great view of the summit of Mount Robson itself, which is quite often obscured by clouds. This brought a fleeting reminiscence of some great backpacking trips, before I forced my mind back to the business at hand.

Our drive next took us along the Fraser River and the 12 km-long (7 mile) Moose Lake, near the end of which was Red Pass – our destination. The highway patrol car was already there, waiting for us.

At the place where we stopped, there was room for a vehicle to pull over, off the highway to the right, and then a mountain rising rapidly beside that. To the left of the highway, there was also a broad shoulder. Down the embankment on that side was a shallow but fairly fast flowing stream – an offshoot of the Fraser River. Across the stream was a rising embankment, beside which ran a set of railway tracks. To the left of the tracks, was another rapidly rising mountain. A short distance ahead of us was the opening to a train tunnel. This was one of the classic Rocky Mountain train tunnels, built in the 1800s and looking like an ageing concrete doorway with an inky black mouth. To the right of the entrance, a gravel and scrub-brush slope descended to meet the running stream. On the left side of the entrance, the terrain was also gravel and scrub-brush for a distance of twenty or thirty feet, then solid forest all the way up the mountainside until rock and gravel made their appearance high up, above the tree-line.

We decided that Jack and I would stakeout this area, while the other two constables would position themselves out of sight near the other end of the train tunnel, a couple of miles away. Jack and I found a trail leading into the right-hand mountain and backed our car into it, making sure it was far enough in so that it wouldn't easily be seen from the highway. It was a tight fit, but we were able to squeeze out of the car, after which Jack, Silver, and I walked back to the highway, across it, and across the stream.

Between the stream and the tracks there were several dense clumps of trees that looked like good vantage points from which we could both hide and observe. Jack chose a spot with the best overall view of the area, taking the risk of possibly not being able to hear much. Silver and I took a position that was as close to the mouth of the tunnel as I thought we could risk. Then, we settled in as best we could. We didn't expect to have long to wait.

I had brought the binoculars with me, and so had the best view of what came next.

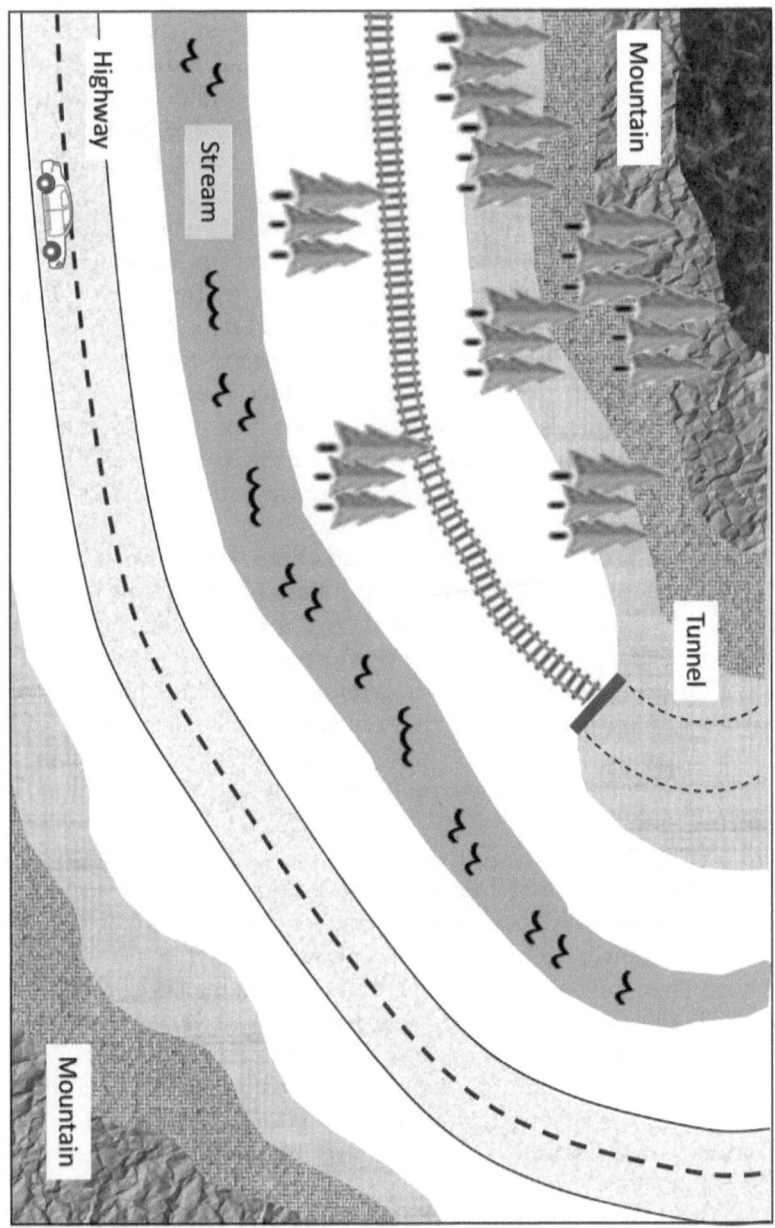

Oliver and Nathan Risk, upon reaching Red Pass, pulled off the highway and parked their car on the shoulder. As they got out, Oliver in particular took a hard look down the highway in both directions. Seeming satisfied, he opened the trunk of the car and extracted the aluminum-frame backpack. Reaching in, he withdrew a folding shovel and a rucksack, the latter of which he passed to Nathan, who was no longer wearing his clerical collar. He did have his bible with him, however, which he placed into the rucksack.

Shouldering their packs, and with Nathan carrying the shovel, Oliver led the way. They crossed the highway, stream, and railway tracks, then approached the tunnel entrance. At this point Oliver took a careful look at the old, concrete-framed tunnel entrance.

"Things look a bit different than they used to," he said.

They were so close to my position that I had little trouble watching and listening, and I kept a hand on Silver so he would know to remain still. I thought that, by then, I had a pretty good idea of what was going to happen next, but there were still some surprises.

"Hand me your bible, Nathan," said Oliver, with his hand out.

Nathan seemed to be as surprised at this as I was, but he took off his rucksack, withdrew and handed over the bible that had never been far from his hands over the previous six days.

With a pocket knife, Oliver carefully slit the stitching of the bible's soft leather cover all the way around the edges, front and back. Handing the bible back to Nathan he said: "Remember I always told you that if anything happened to me, you should look inside your bible? This is why."

"A map!" exclaimed Nathan.

Sure enough, Oliver held open the leather bible cover and they looked at what was drawn on its reverse side. I couldn't see what was written or drawn there, of course, but they studied it for a while. Then Oliver looked around again, as if recalibrating his bearings.

"This way," he said. "Bring your pack."

I was able to observe the two of them scramble up the steep slope on the left side of the train tunnel's concrete opening. When they reached the top of the concrete frame, Oliver stood with his shoes placed right against the frame's top-left corner and said: "Read off the paces."

"Twenty-five left from the edge, keeping to the same elevation as the top of the tunnel... OK, now ten paces to your right, straight up the slope… OK, now…"

I couldn't hear the rest, nor see them anymore. They couldn't have gone much further, though, because a few minutes later I could hear the sounds of digging as they used the shovel to excavate gravel and dirt. The digging sounds went on for a while, until the shovel made a kind of 'clunk' sound. They had struck something.

I could hear the voices of the two of them talking for a while, but couldn't make out any of what they were saying.

Things went completely quiet after that, and after fifteen minutes I was trying to decide whether to risk changing my position or not, when the two of them came back into my line of sight. They had their packs on and were very carefully making their way back down the gravel and scrub-bush covered slope. I judged that their caution was due to their packs being heavier than they were used to. I found out later that Oliver's backpack had become 30 pounds heavier, while the weight of Nathan's had increased by 60 pounds. The shovel, they had simply discarded.

When the two of them reached the clearing in front of the tunnel, they stopped and took their packs off for a few moments rest. Despite the lighter pack, it was Oliver that had tired the most easily, and when he'd recovered his breath he said, "OK, let's get moving again."

As they were about to hoist their packs, they were stopped by a commanding voice coming from the direction of the tunnel:

"Just leave the packs where they are!"

9 SHOWDOWN

When the Peters reached the area of the train tunnel, the Colonel noted the Risks' rental car parked beside the road and kept driving for a few hundred yards before stopping and making a U-turn on the highway. Doubling back, he drove until just before the tunnel entrance and clearing, and parked beside the highway.

Instructing Hannah to remain in the car, he took something from his carry-on bag in the back seat and walked beside the highway towards the clearing. When he rounded the corner, Hannah immediately got out of the car and followed him.

As she walked along the side of the mountain, she came up to the clearing and rounded the corner by the entrance to the train tunnel just in time to hear the Colonel's voice, saying "Just leave the packs where they are!"

***

My hidden vantage point had turned out to be almost perfect. I saw Oliver and Nathan Risk come down the mountain and stop for their brief rest. I saw the Colonel step forward from the shadow of the train tunnel, with a large automatic pistol in his hand. *Probably a military .45 calibre,* I thought.

I also saw Hannah come around the corner in time to be able to take in the whole scene for herself as well.

The brief silence was broken not by the Risks, who stood there for a moment, scowling, but by Hannah.

"Dad, what's going on? Why do you have a gun? And what are Nathan and his dad doing here?"

"I told you to stay in the car!" the Colonel barked. "Now that you're here, stay where you are and don't interfere…." While saying this, he hadn't taken his eyes away from Oliver and Nathan, nor had his gun – which was pointed at them – wavered at all.

"Who the hell are you?" asked Oliver.

"Just someone with an interest in the gold, that's all… take your gun out and toss it over to me."

Oliver visibly hesitated.

"Don't try to bluff me. You wouldn't have come here without a gun. I want it now!"

Then, as Oliver reluctantly reached into his jacket pocket, the Colonel spoke sharply and warningly: "Carefully now. I'll start by shooting your son if I have to."

Continuing to scowl, Oliver carefully withdrew a revolver from his jacket and carefully tossed it over to the Colonel.

"OK, now back away from the packs."

When they did so, the Colonel called out to his daughter. "Hannah, now that you're here anyway, come and take one of these packs."

As Hannah stood frozen in place, the Colonel moved quickly to pick up Oliver's gun and put it in his own pocket. With his gun hand covering the Risks, he used his free hand to experimentally heft the two packs. Finding what appeared to be the heaviest one, he grabbed one of the shoulder straps and one-handed it up and onto one shoulder.

"Who are you, anyway?" croaked Oliver Risk.

"Why Jon, I'm surprised you don't remember me. After all these years, I certainly still remember you!"

As Oliver just stood there, looking confused, the Colonel continued. "No? Let me give you another hint. We were partners once upon a time. You had the brains and I had the dynamite. Does that help?"

"Slim?" said Oliver, disbelievingly. "But you can't be…" his voice trailed off.

"Why not, because I'm dead? Because you killed my brother and me inside that tunnel 58 years ago? Well, you shot both of us in there all right, and then took the gold and rode off, leaving us to die. Except that I didn't die. I don't know why.

"I was unconscious at first. When I came to, you were gone. I crawled over to my brother, who was alive but in bad shape. As I lay there holding my brother in my arms while he died, I wanted to join him. But I didn't die, and when they came and found us still lying there together, they took my brother and buried him somewhere while I ended up under guard in a hospital, until I was well enough to go to jail.

"Meanwhile you had taken off with the loot... Hannah, get over here. What are you doing?" he asked, without taking his eyes off of the Risks.

Hannah hadn't moved. "Dad! What is all this? What are you doing?"

"I'll explain it all to you later. For now, just come and get the rucksack and we'll leave. No one will get hurt... no one besides Jon - or Oliver - there, that is, and I'll tell you all about it after we've left."

Reluctantly, Hannah went over and picked up the rucksack, then walked over to the front of the train tunnel and stopped again. Still hesitant, she took off the pack and put it back down on the ground, then stood there staring at her father.

"Now what?" demanded the Colonel.

"This feels wrong Dad. Like stealing. What's in these packs? What has any of this got to do with us? And why are you threatening these people?"

"I said I'll tell you about it later. Now do as I say. Lift that pack up, and let's get out of here!"

"No, Dad. I don't know what's in here that's so important to you, or why everyone seems to have guns, but we can't just steal stuff from Nathan and his father."

"Hannah, I'm telling you for the last time. Bring that pack over here or I'll take it away myself and leave you here."

"Dad!"

"I mean it. Make your choice. You're either with me or you're with them!"

Hannah just continued to stand there, but visibly shaking now. It was obvious that strong emotions and uncertainties were swirling inside her.

"Hannah can just stand still where she is," said a new voice.

***

Ben, who had been following the Peters, kept going when he saw the Colonel make a U-turn. He continued past them and drive on for another mile, then made his own U-turn and drove slowly back. By the time he had a clear view of the Peter's car, the Colonel was already walking away and Hannah was just getting out, in contravention of her father's instructions.

Ben slowed down.

Only when Hannah turned the mountain's corner, and went out of sight, did Ben pick up speed, driving until he reached the Peters' car, then pulled his pickup truck in behind it. Exiting the truck and closing its door very quietly, Ben jogged ahead to the edge of the mountain that Hannah had disappeared behind.

Crouching low, he peered around the corner and was just in time to hear the Colonel identify himself as a former partner of Oliver and pocket the latter's gun. When the Colonel demanded for the second time that Hannah pick up a pack and help him, Ben took his cue.

"Hannah can just stand still where she is," said Ben.

Even the Colonel was startled into turning his head, just as Ben quickly darted forward to reach Hannah and grab her arm. In his other hand he held a gun, too.

I think everyone except Jack and I were surprised to see Ben appear. Of the rest, Hannah was the first speak up.

"Ben! What are you doing here? What's going on?"

"I think I'm here for the same reason your father is, and it's not to see the sights," said Ben. "I'll tell you about it later, if you want, but for now, just stand here quietly with me.... Well, Colonel? How about tossing both guns over here?"

As they stared at each other, the Colonel spoke. "Look son, let me give you some military advice. Number one, that little revolver of yours has nowhere near the destructive power of my army .45.

"Number two, I'm a better shot that you are, so while you may or may not be able to hit me, I most certainly will not miss hitting you.

"Number three, if you shoot or otherwise hurt Hannah, I will put all seven rounds into you.

"Number four, even if you manage to hit me, it will take several shots to take down a man of my size and determination, whereas I will most certainly shoot you dead.

"So, my advice to you is to toss your little gun over to me, and you can walk away from this and live to fight another day. Now that's sound tactical advice, but it's entirely up to you. What do you say?"

"I want to know what happened to the loot," said Ben, angrily and with Hannah positioned in front of him as a shield.

"Don't ask me," said the Colonel calmly. "Ask him," he motioned with his gun towards Oliver.

"You know him as Oliver Risk. I knew him as Jon Hope the outlaw and leader of our little gang. I was a member, and so was my brother Jess. We stopped a train and robbed it, right over there," he pointed along the tracks, a short distance away.

"After the robbery, the three of us each took part of the loot and rode into the tunnel, planning to come out the other side and make our way to the coast. From there we were going to take a liner down the U.S. to San Francisco, to hide out.

"But Jon tricked us. When we entered the tunnel, our eyes were still adjusting to the darkness when he shot us down, just inside the entrance there. Then the bastard left us for dead, except I pulled through.

"It took me a long, long time to recover, serve my time in jail, serve in a couple of wars, and then, finally, I got my life's wish: I found out where he was hiding in the States, and the name he'd assumed: Oliver Risk."

The Colonel paused a moment, as if remembering.

"But he took all the loot. Like I said, after getting shot I was unconscious for a while. Maybe that and the blood are why he thought I was dead. Anyway, he didn't take our horses. Maybe he thought it would be too conspicuous, I don't know. Whatever the reason, part of it was in gold coins. The gold was too heavy for him and his horse to carry, so he hid it around here somewhere.

"The rest of the loot was paper money. He must have taken with him. As near as I can tell, he spent the money over the years, went into debt, and came back here to get the gold...

"Now. How did you find out about it? And who the hell are you anyway?"

Somewhat reluctantly, Ben picked up the tale from there.

"There weren't three people in the gang back then, there were four. My father was Robert Shaw, the fourth member, and what they called 'the man on the inside.'

"It was my father that that tipped off the others about the train's route and schedule, the express car's contents, and the fact that a particular run had less than the usual number of guards and no alarms installed.

"And my father got cheated too. Jon Hope high-tailed it for the U.S. without ever handing over my father's share of the loot, and my father died just around the time he finally tracked him down.

"He knew all about you though. Before he died, he told me all about the robbery, and the gang, and the loot. Because he worked for the bank, he knew that the gold coins had never surfaced, and he knew that only one horse had been ridden away, so he figured that the paper money was gone but that coins must have been hidden around here somewhere.

"He knew, through the bank, that some of the paper money had been spent in the southern U.S., and in little bits at a time, although that knowledge hadn't helped the police to track him down. He also knew that your brother hadn't survived, of course, but he followed your career closely. So closely that he even knew about your efforts to find Jon Hope, including that you found him and turned his secretary into a double agent."

There was a pause as he looked closely at the Colonel's face.

"I see that surprises you. Here's another surprise. You were paying his secretary to keep you informed about Jon Hope's business travels, which is how you knew exactly when and how he was going to come back to Canada and then all the way across the country to this place. What you didn't know, is that my dad bribed the same secretary into becoming a triple agent. Every time he sent you a report on Jon Hope's travel plans, he sent the same information to my dad and got paid all over again for the same information.

"My dad died recently, but not before the last report came in. The one about his plans to come to Canada and come all the way west. His train ticket was good all the way to Vancouver, but I figured – just like you did – that his real plan was to get off the train and find his way here.

"I didn't know where he'd hidden the loot, so I just followed you while you followed him.... So, you see, my father found him by following you, and I found the loot by following you. Satisfied?"

"I remember your father," the Colonel said, reflectively. "He seemed like a good man. The authorities thought there must have been an inside man on the job, and they tried to make me give him up. Even promised me a lighter sentence. But I never did..."

He shook himself out of his reminiscences. "Look, I have no grudge against you, and now you know that you should have no grudge against me, otherwise your father would have gone to jail like I did. How about if you take the other pack that's lying there and walk away. Hannah and I will do the same with this one and we can go our separate ways."

"What about those two?" asked Ben, nodding towards Oliver Risk (a.k.a. Jon Hope) and his son.

"If it wasn't for Hannah being here, I'd say let's just kill them both and move along, but she'd never forgive me for that and I guess I don't have anything against the reverend there. We could each shoot Jon in a leg though. At least he'd spend the rest of his life in misery that way."

No one said anything for a moment, but Ben's gun slowly moved to point toward Oliver (Jon), and likewise did the Colonel's gun.

Time to step in, I thought. I hoped I knew what I was doing.

"That's a horrible choice you offered Hannah a moment ago, you know," I said as Silver and I stepped out from the small cluster of trees behind which we'd been hiding. My service revolver was pointed towards both the Colonel and Ben, but I was speaking to the Colonel.

"On the one hand, she loves you and feels a duty to you as her father; on the other hand, she has correctly sensed that something very wrong is going on here. Making things worse for her are the feelings she's obviously developed for Nathan there, and maybe even for Ben."

"And you think you know what's going on?" The big .45 revolver was pointing at me now.

"Yes, I think I do. If you drop that gun I'll explain."

His gun didn't waver until Silver, without needing to be told, started shifting himself sideways so he'd be able to come at the Colonel from the side if he needed to.

The Colonel was experienced enough to immediately recognize a flanking maneuvre, of course. "Keep that dog away from me or I'll kill him," he barked.

"Colonel, that's a police dog doing his job. If you shoot at him, you will be shot yourself."

"By you?" he said, disbelievingly.

"Without hesitation. I hope you can believe that. But before you decide, let me give you some police advice, just like the military advice you offered earlier for Ben over there.

"Point number one, my revolver doesn't have quite as much destructive power as yours does, but it's more than enough to seriously wound or kill you.

"Point number two: mine's fully loaded and I don't think Ben's a killer, so I really only have one target to worry about: you." I hoped I was right about Ben.

"Point number three, I might not be a better shot than you are, but at this range, it won't matter much.

"Point number four: just like you said, even if you manage to hit me, it will take several shots to take me down, meaning that I'll get a couple of shots in too.

"Point number five, there's Silver to consider. He's faced men with guns before, and he's even been shot before. He won't hurt you unless I ask him to, but I need to warn you that he and I aren't just partners, we're close friends. What that means is that if you shoot me, he will attack you. Even if I ask him not to, he will attack you. Of course, he won't kill you... but Jack might."

"Jack?" he quickly glanced around, warily.

"Yes, my colleague, Constable Jack McDonald." I waved vaguely over my shoulder towards another clump of trees, behind me. A quick glance confirmed that Jack had been listening closely, and had taken his cue and stepped out from the trees, immediately dropped to one knee, and shouldered a rifle.

"Drop the gun Colonel," he ordered.

"So. That makes six reasons," I continued. "Any one of them by themselves might not be convincing, but take them all together... I think that sound military strategy would call for a surrender in this case. Wouldn't you?"

He hesitated.

"At this point, you may be thinking that Mounties won't shoot first. That's generally true, and we might just let you get the first shot off. But what then? If you shoot one of us, the other will certainly shoot you, and despite what you might think from Mountie fiction, we're not trained to shoot to wound."

Still the Colonel hesitated, and it felt like a frozen moment in time.

Perhaps it was because no one was speaking, but I suddenly heard a new sound layered over the background sounds of the running stream beside us. It took me a moment to figure out what the sound was. It sounded faintly mechanical. Something about it made me glance towards the tunnel entrance. Then I saw the light.

Oh no!

The others must have seen the direction of my glance, or perhaps the expression on my face, but before any of us could do anything, nothing could take precedence over the locomotive's five-chime horn.

I actually went and looked it up later. Under Transport Canada regulations, Canada's train locomotives must be equipped with a dual-tone horn located in an unobstructed location near the front of the roof, facing the direction of travel, and capable of producing a soft 'normal' sound, and a loud 'emergency' sound. Well, the locomotive's engineer must have seen us near the mouth of the tunnel, because they had pulled the cord for the emergency sound.

A five-chime locomotive horn under emergency air pressure is designed to get people's attention, and has to be at least 96 decibels at a distance of 30 metres (100 feet) away. For us, standing within about 10 metres (30 feet) of the emerging locomotive it was deafening – like standing next to a jackhammer.

It certainly made me jump!

The problem with the train was that Jack, Silver, and I were on the 'stream' side of the tracks, while everyone else was on the 'mountain' side. And, of course, it had to be a freight train. It had three locomotives and more than sixty cars, giving it a total length of something like one-and-a-half kilometres (nearly a mile). Coming, as it was, out of a tunnel, it was moving fairly slowly too.

I thought I heard gunshots, but there was nothing we could do but wait.

Laurie Schramm

10 ESCAPE

On the 'mountain' side of the tracks the Colonel, of course, was the first to unfreeze. Boldly striding forward, he moved closer to Ben and Hannah, took careful aim, and shot Ben in his gun arm.

The force of the high-calibre slug spun Ben nearly 45 degrees to one side and dropped him to his knees. It also caused him to drop the gun he was holding, and to release Hannah so he could press his other hand against his bleeding arm.

Sprinting the last few yards, the Colonel swiftly picked up Ben's gun, pocketed it, and used his own gun to deliver a punishing blow to Ben's head. Stunned, Ben dropped like a stone.

Ignoring him, the Colonel reached over and took Hanna's arm.

"No time to debate this, Hannah. You need to come with me now, and I promise I'll explain everything later – right?"

"I don't understand any of this," she said, shakily.

"Just pick up that pack, like I told you, and follow me." As Hannah tentatively made to go and pick up the rucksack, the Colonel strode over to where Oliver (a.k.a. Jon) and Nathan were still standing.

"All right you two. Hannah and I are leaving with the gold, and you two are going to stay right here, yes?"

Nathan's response was to open his bible, as if to cite some passage that would make the Colonel change his mind.

The Colonel looked at him in disbelief and disdain. "Freeze. Don't make any moves at all!"

Before Nathan could decide what to do next, Oliver tried to take advantage of the distraction and lunged at the Colonel, as if trying to get at the gun he was holding. If that was his intention, he had badly miscalculated as he was too far away. Before he could even get close, the Colonel simply aimed and fired, bringing Oliver down into a collapsed heap, holding the leg where he'd been hit.

Nathan's reaction was instantaneous. Dropping the bible, he went to help his father.

Still angry at Oliver's foolish attempt, the Colonel's first impulse was to raise his left hand as if to physically attack Nathan, but then his professional instincts took over and, realizing that Nathan wasn't a serious threat, simply snarled "Look after your father."

Stepping over to Hannah, he went to help her finish putting on the rucksack, but she backed away as if afraid of him. "Look Dad, I don't care what you did when you were young, but you know better now. You've hurt these people — we have to stay here and help them."

"Help them!" the Colonel was incredulous. "Jon there is lucky I didn't kill him, and Ben there got what he deserves for trying to interfere with me!"

"No, Dad. It's wrong… You go if you want, but I'm going to stay here and help them."

"Hannah, I told you to come or I'd leave you here. Decide now!"

But Hannah had already made her decision. Visibly shaking, but standing her ground, she said, defiantly, "Go then. I'm staying here to help them."

The Colonel stared at her for a moment, then came to a decision. "Fine then. Have it your own way." The larger backpack was still on one shoulder. Switching his gun to his left hand, and keeping a close eye on the Risks, he slipped the other strap up and over his right shoulder. Then, switching his gun over again, he picked up the rucksack in his left hand and jogged toward the mountainside path that the Risks had descended earlier.

As Hannah ran to help Nathan and his father, the Colonel began climbing the mountain and disappeared into the forest.

By this time, Nathan had made a quick inspection of his father and discovered that Oliver's leg was bleeding from a point on his front thigh, and another on the back side.

"Looks like the bullet went straight through," he said to both his father and Hannah, who had rushed over. "That's a good sign. We just have to stop the bleeding." Stripping off his light jacket and taking out a pocketknife, he cut each jacket sleeve off and tied them together. Then, he rolled-up the rest of the jacket and wrapped it around his father's injured leg as a makeshift bandage. Using the tied jacket sleeves like a strap, he wrapped it around the jacket and tied it in place. Then, he looked Hannah straight in the eyes. "Would you do something for me?" he asked.

It all took place in about five minutes, after which the train had passed them by, on its way east.

***

Once the train had passed, Silver and I crossed the tracks, followed, not far behind, by Jack. I was closest to Ben, so I ran to where he lay, while Jack ran over to Oliver and Hannah.

Ben was barely conscious and lying in a pool of blood, his eyes unfocused. His pulse was strong though, and as I checked him over it seemed like the blood was all coming from his right arm. I gave him a full pat-down anyway, looking for weapons, but only found a pocketknife.

Turning my focus back to his injury, I had a bandanna in one pocket, which I took out and tied around his arm to slow the bleeding. As I tied the bandanna, Ben seemed to come out of his stupor and I could see the exact moment when his mind cleared and the pain hit.

"He shot me and then he hit me," said Ben, in a shaky voice.

"Who did?"

"The Colonel."

"OK, just sit here quietly for a moment while I go check on the others, then we'll radio in for some help."

By the time I had walked over to Jack, he had just checked over Nathan's first aid work.

"Looks like the bullet went right through. Mr. Risk looks a bit shaky and is pain, but I don't think the bullet did more than graze the bone as it went past, so he should be OK."

"How many shots did you hear?" I asked Jack.

He thought for a moment. "Sounded like two. Large calibre."

"Me too," I agreed.

Stepping back a couple of feet, I looked pointedly at Oliver and Hannah. "Where's the gun?"

Silence.

"If you want our help, you need to tell me where the gun is… and where are the Colonel and Nathan?"

"Dad has a gun. Ben and Mr. Risk both had guns too, but dad has them as well." Hannah then related what had happened on their side of the freight train, finishing up with: "…and then Nathan asked me to look after his father while he went after Dad and the gold."

"That's crazy," Jack exclaimed. "Your father has already shot two people and is on the run with stolen gold and, according to you, he has three guns with him. What does Nathan think he's going to be able to do?"

"I don't know," said Hannah, breaking into tears now. "But he does have a gun. I saw him take it out of his bible and put it in his pocket before he left," she said, pointing vaguely to one side.

There, lying open but upside down on the ground, was Nathan's bible. When I went over to pick it up and turned it over in my hands, the bible was half open. The right-hand pages had been hollowed out in the approximate shape of a gun.

My jaw dropped in surprise. *Nathan had a gun?* I thought.

"Look at this, Jack."

"Must be a small one. About the size of a derringer, wouldn't you say?"

I nodded. It looked exactly right for a derringer. I knew, because I sometimes carried one myself, when working undercover. "OK, so he's armed, but he's probably only got two rounds – he'll be hopelessly outgunned."

Suddenly, we heard the *Crack!* of a gunshot.

"What was that," cried Hannah.

"One of them took a shot," said Jack.

"You'll stop them, won't you?" asked Hannah, still sniffling from shock and stress. "You won't let Dad hurt him?"

"We'll certainly do our best, Hannah. But first, we need to look after Mr. Risk and Ben. Then, we'll see what we can do."

Leaving Silver and I to keep an eye on things, Jack ran down to the highway and our unmarked police car to radio for the highway patrol car, which was still at the other stakeout position at the far end of the tunnel, to come help. The he ran back, bringing with him the police car's first aid kit.

As we cleaned and properly bandaged Oliver Risk's leg and Ben's arm, we verified that, in both cases, the slugs had gone right through. We couldn't, however, judge how much internal damage the slugs had done along the way. By then, Ben had regained consciousness, and both he and Hannah wanted to know how we had known to be there.

Since we had a few minutes before help arrived, I told them some more of the story.

"As you both know now, right about here, back in 1920, three men robbed a train: Jon Hope – also known as Oliver Risk, Slim Peters, - also known as Colonel James Peters, and Slim's brother Jess.

"I'm told that the robbery went like clockwork, and that the three men robbed the train of $44,000 in only 45 minutes. Of the loot, $20,000 was in banknotes, and the other $24,000 was in gold coins.

"That was a lot of money back in 1920. In today's dollars, the paper currency would be worth about $66,000, with inflation. But the gold is worth a lot more now that it was back then, about $220,000."

At this point there was an audible gasp from Ben, but if he had a question, he was pre-empted by Hannah.

"Who cares about a robbery that happened nearly sixty years ago?" she asked.

"Actually quite a few people care, really," I continued. "In the first place, very little of the loot was ever recovered. You already know that some of the paper money had been spent in the southern U.S., and in little bits at a time. It's assumed that more of the paper currency was spent in other places, also in relatively small amounts at a time, that was never identified with the train robbery.

"The gold, on the other hand, was in the form of Dominion of Canada, George V, $5 and $10 coins issued between 1912 and 1914. Now, the interesting thing about the coins is that partway through 1914, Canada was preparing for the First World War and it stopped selling gold coins and began hoarding gold instead. That made the coins fairly rare by 1920, and anyone trying to sell more than a couple of them would look suspicious to the banks, who were on the alert.

If any of the rare coins had shown up, they would certainly have been noticed.

"Now, we had no way of knowing for sure, but the Force always thought that the gold was hidden away somewhere: either where it was originally hidden or somewhere else. Jon Hope had ambushed his partners in the tunnel there, presumably under the cover of the darkness, and left them for dead. He also left their horses behind, probably thinking they'd be too conspicuous, but that left him with a problem: his horse couldn't carry him plus all the loot. It was thought that he hid the gold, which would have weighed 90 pounds, and took the currency, which would have weighed only 40 pounds, and which would have been easier to spend if he was careful. And it seems he was very careful.

"Of course, as we found out today, the gold was buried just up there, in the side of this mountain, and if it was all here it will be in 9 or 10 bags, in those two packs that the Colonel took.

"Anyway, getting back to 'who cares,' the Bank of Canada would still like to have the gold recovered, which is reason number one, and they want the thieves caught and tried, which is reason number two."

"Isn't there some kind of statute of limitations on that sort of thing?" asked Ben.

"You may be thinking of American law. In Canada, there is no statute of limitations under the Criminal Code for indictable offenses like major theft, and don't forget murder.

"So, reason number three is murder. Now Jon, that is, Oliver here, might not realize this, being American, but we in Canada take murder very seriously and – just like they say in all the Mountie novels and movies – once we're on a murderer's trail we never give up. There's been an outstanding warrant for the arrest of Jonathan Hope for 58 years now."

"I thought you said you were checking out security on the train for a VIP trip that was coming up," said Hannah.

"That's actually quite true. Jack and Silver and I have been diligently making notes on security strengths and weaknesses along this whole trip. But we've had another mission too. To explain that, I need to go back to your father's story.

"As you heard, your father recovered from the ambush and was caught and hospitalized. After spending a year recovering from two near-fatal gunshot wounds, he was tried, convicted and sentenced to

15 years. It was a high sentence because the gang had used dynamite in the robbery, and he was the dynamite expert. He was released in 1928, after having served seven years of his sentence, but he immediately joined another gang, got caught robbing a bank – using dynamite again – and people in the bank got shot, so his next sentence was higher: 20 years. He served eight years of that sentence, then was then paroled in 1938."

This started Hannah sobbing again, although she kept listening, despite the imagery of having placed both hands over her ears.

"After his second release from jail, your father seemed to finally decide to 'go straight' and you probably know most of the rest. Using his proper first name, James, he enlisted in the army - specializing in demolitions, of course. He served in the Second World War from 1939 to 1945, got married in 1946, then served in the Korean war from 1950 to 1953, and retired in 1954. From there, he went into a civilian demolition business. You, Hannah, were born in 1960, and your father retired again in 1968.

"Your father knew that Jon had gotten away, and it seems he tried hard to find him, although we don't know whether that was a long-term thing or a recent thing. Meanwhile my boss, or at least my boss and his predecessors, had been trying to locate Jonathan Hope as well. With the help of the FBI, they finally located him, but only recently.

"It turns out that Jonathan Hope used some or all of the stolen money to became Oliver Risk and establish himself as a businessman in the southern United States. He married late in life, but his wife died young, leaving him to raise their only son, Nathan Risk. He seems to have done fairly well in business, but his business began to falter in the 1970s, leaving it near bankruptcy earlier this year. On top of that, the FBI discovered that he had been siphoning-off company funds for many years. So, this year, finding himself in desperate need of money again, and possibly worried that his company's bankruptcy would expose his fraudulent activities, he decided to come back for the gold…. Any comment Mr. Hope?"

"No," was all he said.

"Well, Nathan had been studying at a divinity college in Halifax. When he graduated and was ordained in the church, he phoned and told Nathan that he wanted to celebrate by driving up to Canada and taking him on a father-son trip across Canada. He 'always wanted to see Canada,' he said to him…"

"How the hell did you know that?" spoke up Jon (Oliver), in spite of himself.

"The FBI were already investigating you for fraud, and they had a wiretap on your phone. They passed on the details to us, so we knew which train you were going to take and when. Unfortunately, this was all very recent, so we didn't have a current photo of you yet, only a description. That's why, I didn't know who you were until we met as we boarded the train in Halifax. There was only one elderly man travelling with a newly minted minister."

"How did Dad find him then?" Hannah asked.

"We don't know. It's possible he maintained some underworld connections. We think he probably used private detectives but, in any case, he finally located Jon in the U.S., going under the name Oliver Risk. Figuring that Oliver would probably return for the gold one day, he managed to meet Oliver's executive secretary, and arranged to secretly pay him to pass on advance details every time Jon (Oliver) went on a trip. It paid off this year, when Oliver asked his secretary to book a trip to Canada. The secretary promptly informed the Colonel of the trip and its itinerary, which is how he ended up on this same train ride across Canada. We know all this, because the FBI had wiretaps on the secretary's office phone and also his personal phone."

"How did you find out?" asked Jon (Oliver).

"Once my boss knew that Jon Hope had become Oliver Risk, and had learned that both Oliver and the Colonel had tickets booked on the same train trip across Canada, he was sure he knew where that would lead, so he sent Jack, Silver, and I to keep an eye on you."

"Were you watching me then, too?" asked Ben.

"No, not at first. But it didn't take long to discover that, while the Colonel was keeping an eye on the Risks, you were always there watching the Risks too. At first, I didn't know whether you were also watching the Colonel, or maybe just watching a pretty girl in the form of Hannah here, but over time it seemed like you were watching all of them. I asked my boss to try to find out who you were, but it took them a long time. It was only late in the evening, when we were in Edmonton, that I received a message saying that our people had made a connection between you and your father, and between him and the train robbery. That gave us a possible reason for your interest.

"Then there were the break-ins. I was pretty sure that they were the work of the same person but in different disguises. The VIA Rail people found the nun's habit you threw out the window, because it got caught on a projection from the Park Dome Car and was noticed hanging there at the next station stop. That was just bad luck. Your only real mistake was dropping the VIA Rail Tie when we were stopped in Winnipeg.

"I kept both of them, and later asked Silver to track the scent. I expected him to lead me to Hannah, whom I suspected might be in league with her father.

"I was wrong, though. Silver led me to your room, Ben. Your disguises were perfect, but they couldn't fool Silver because he tracks people by their scent. Of course, by that time, you'd abruptly left the train."

"How did you know that the gold would be hidden here?" asked Hannah.

"We didn't, but we knew where the train robbery occurred, and the most likely places to hide the loot would have been near one or the other of the entrances to this train tunnel. That's why there's a police car at the other end: we had two people at each entrance."

"So this was all about revenge?" asked Hannah, looking disdainfully at Ben."

"Revenge and money. My father knew all about money. Those packs hold 1,200 $10 coins and 2,400 $5 coins. They are all George V coins, minted between 1912 and 1914. In today's dollars, the gold value is over $217,000, but they're also very rare, so they're worth more than that to collectors. Anyone possessing them would be instantly wealthy, and for life."

"And Dad's a fanatical coin collector!" breathed Hannah.

"Really? Well, then he knows their value too."

At this point, we were interrupted by the sound of a wailing siren and the approach of the highway patrol car that had been stationed at the far end of the tunnel. Given that we were an hour's drive from the nearest small hospital, which was in Jasper, the two constables agreed to take Oliver and Ben by police car, rather than wait for an ambulance to come all the way out and back, which would have doubled the time needed to get the two injured people there. Hannah wanted to go with them, which was just as well since Jack, Silver, and I had other things to do.

Oliver Risk (Jon Hope) was arrested on the outstanding warrant, with more charges to follow. We had to arrest Ben too, of course, for threatening people with a restricted weapon, the theft of the truck, and the three earlier break-ins on the train. Oliver was placed in the back of the unmarked station wagon, lying on some folded blankets with his hands cuffed in front of him, then one constable sat with a handcuffed Ben in the back seat, while the other constable drove, with Hannah in the front passenger seat.

Tossing the magnetic-base, flashing-red light up on the roof, and with the siren actuated, they took off for Jasper leaving us with the marked-highway-patrol car and a promise to radio in for extra backup for us.

Then it was time for us to track down the Colonel and see if we could prevent Nathan from any further foolishness.

11 THE CHASE IS ON

Before trading cars, Jack and I had pulled all of our luggage out of the station-wagon to make room for Oliver (Jon) to be put in the back. As we put them in the trunk of the highway patrol car, I pulled a daypack out of one of my bags and stuffed in a light jacket, flashlight, and two large bottles of water that I'd purchased in Jasper. The Jasper Detachment had also loaned us two handheld, Motorola MX300, VHF police radios. They were bulky and heavy, weighing nearly a kilogram (2 pounds), I was going to need one, so I attached the radio to the front of one shoulder strap and the microphone to the other strap.

When I was ready, we looked across the stream and tracks to the mountainside.

"Which way do you think" asked Jack.

"I think the Colonel's crazy to run at all… but if it was me, I'd look for game trails and try to make my way west, following the train tunnel from above, then drop down to the highway at the other end. He may have been up there watching the others being taken away, in which case he'll probably guess that it's just you, Silver, and I that he has to worry about for the next hour until we get backup. He's probably too smart to come back for his rental car, so maybe he'll pretend to be a tourist backpacker and try hitch-hiking?"

"Sounds reasonable. How about if you go see if Silver can find their scent and I'll wait here? Once you're sure which way they're going, radio me and I'll pace you from the highway with the car."

"Agreed. Come Silver. Time to hunt."

"*Grruph!*"

After Silver and I had re-crossed the highway, stream, and railroad tracks, I checked my watch as we looked up at the mountain beside and above the railway tunnel: it was just about 1 pm and the Colonel had about an hour's lead on us.

Spotting Nathan's bible on the ground, I picked it up. Crouching down on one knee, I took Silver's face in my hands and looked deeply into his eyes. "Remember Nathan, Silver? Track Nathan..." and I gave him the bible to sniff. Although the leather cover/map had been cut away, it was still wrapped around the bible and should have been a good source of scent, I thought, given that it was seldom out of Nathan's hands.

Silver gave it several careful sniffs, then went into tracking mode. Without hesitation went over to the exact spot where Nathan had been tending to his father, sniffed around as if to confirm his scent, then went straight to where the rucksack had originally been lying and did the same thing. Seemingly satisfied, he straightened up, gave me a very direct look, and then started making his way to the side of the tunnel and the faint path leading up the mountainside.

Following him, I had no trouble making out footprints here and there, where there were patches of dirt and shale dust in among the rock and scrub brush.

I don't know whether Silver was following the main overlay of scents at first, or whether he could pick out Nathan's scent from the others, but he led me quite directly to the spot where Oliver and Nathan had been digging. There was a rough hole, perhaps two to three feet below grade, several piles of rubble that had been excavated, and the collapsible shovel that I had watched Oliver take from his backpack some two hours earlier. Off to one side, and barely visible among the rock, brush, and grasses were two axes and a prybar, all very old-looking, with the metal parts heavily rusted and pitted. *The original tools from the train robbery*, I thought.

At this point, Silver circled the whole area, then zig-zagged slightly east and mostly uphill. Just when I'd become convinced that the trail was going to actually lead us to the east, we encountered a game trail that crossed our path. It looked well and recently used, with noticeable piles of fresh-looking mule deer droppings, and it seemed to extend for some distance to our right and to our left, before disappearing into the trees in each direction. Silver went a few feet to the right, sniffing carefully, then returned and went a few feet to the left, sniffing again, then lifted his head and looked meaningfully to the back to the right, as if to say *"That way."*

"Find Nathan," was all I said, and he resumed tracking, heading west and into the trees. As I followed, I turned my radio on and said: "Jack? 10-23[15], heading west."

"10-4[16] Alex. I'll parallel you and advance 150 metres. Let me know if he changes direction."

"OK, I'm going 10-7[17]." That was to let him know that I'd be switching off the radio for a while. I wasn't worried about eavesdroppers, being on a restricted tactical frequency in the middle of the mountains, but I didn't want any radio messages or static to alert the Colonel to my presence if we got close to them.

Motioning for Silver to continue, we advanced.

I didn't actually expect to catch either the Colonel or Nathan on the trail. Although the Colonel would have had his own problems trying to find his way along while being weighted down with heavy packs, Silver and I could only advance at a pace that allowed Silver to keep following the scent. This took a lot of zig-zagging, sweeping in arcs, and occasionally going in complete circles so that, although he never lost the scent for long, we only advanced slowly.

After about 30 minutes of tracking, Silver found several places of interest in a small clearing. Looking closely at the spots that most attracted Silver's attention, I could see scuff marks on the ground, and places where the grasses and low brush had been compressed, by the rucksack.

Turning my radio back on, I called Jack. "Our 10-20[18] is about half a mile, and I think we've found where they stopped for a break. I can see where he put the packs when he set them down."

"10-4," crackled Jack's voice over the radio. "Heading?"

"West, as we thought. Unless something changes, let's meet at the west end of the tunnel."

"10-4. Out."

As Silver continued tracking, there came a time when I heard a train horn give a succession of short blasts.

It took us another 30 minutes to reach a junction with a trail branch heading down the slope. It was 2 pm. Silver very decisively followed the downward branch and we quickly emerged from the forest. Looking down, I could see that we had passed the tunnel opening by about 30 metres (30 yards). Directly below us, railroad tracks emerged from the tunnel. Close beside the track was the same rippling stream as before but, at this end of the tunnel, the highway was much further away from the stream. Pulled over onto the shoulder of the highway was the highway patrol car. Of the Colonel and Nathan, there was no sign.

I motioned for Silver to continue tracking and he led directly along the new path, which took us through several switch-backs as it led down the steep slope, then we were finally on clear, level ground again. At this point Silver angled vaguely westward and almost diagonally toward the tracks. When we reached the tracks, he carefully sniffed his way along one side of the track, then retraced his steps, still sniffing, then he sat down on his haunches – right beside the track- and stared at me.

The scent trail had ended.

Suddenly, I knew what they had done

Damn!

***

The Colonel had climbed the mountain slope as quickly as he could, found the spot where Oliver and Nathan had dug up the gold, and paused to look down. From this vantage point he could see Oliver (Jon), Hannah, and the two police constables, but there was no sign of Nathan.

Damn! *he thought.*

Anger and frustration dominated his emotions, but he was still too much the soldier to let emotion get in the way of strategy and tactics. He would have to keep going and make the assumption that Nathan was in pursuit. Taking one of the smaller caliber guns from his pocket, he fired a shot, vaguely aiming back the way he had come. He had no expectation of hitting Nathan, if he was really back there, just of forcing him to take cover and then proceed slowly, if at all.

There was a slight indication of a trail leading up the mountain slope. He followed it until it intersected a game trail, one branch of which led west. That was the direction he wanted to go. Eventually, he came to a small clearing and decided to take a brief rest. Placing the rucksack on the ground, he also shed the external-frame backpack he'd been wearing.

Allowing himself only a few minutes, he took up the backpack and looked hard at the rucksack. In order to make better time, he decided to abandon the latter. Continuing west, he forced himself to a faster pace.

Before long, there was a junction with a well-worn trail leading down the slope. Heading down, he soon emerged from the forest. There, down and to his right, was a set of railroad tracks and the western end of the tunnel. Next to the tracks was the stream and, further away, was the highway.

Being careful not to trip, he moved down the slope as quickly as possible then jogged to the tracks. He was about to cross the tracks, thinking to ford the stream and try hitchhiking on the highway when he heard a soft mechanical sound echoing from the tunnel.

Smiling grimly, he changed direction and jogged along the side of the tracks, moving away from the tunnel and towards the place where the clearing turned to dense forest.

The sounds of the approaching train were getting louder, and he could just see some light from the locomotive's powerful headlights being reflected along one tunnel wall as he dug out from his pocket a red bandanna.

What a day to have picked a red one, *he thought as he began waving it over his head, just as the locomotive emerged from the tunnel.*

***

The engineer and conductor of the freight train were seated, one on each side, looking ahead as the locomotive emerged from the train tunnel. As a result, they both spotted the figure waving a red flag at the same time.

"Something wrong up ahead," said the conductor.

Nodding, the engineer jerked the cord for the train's horn so it gave a succession of short blasts — a warning that the train was preparing to stop.

***

As soon as he heard the horn blasts from the train, the Colonel stopped waving his bandanna and tucked it back into his pocket. Crouched low, he ran to the forest fringe and hid behind the nearest trees.

***

As the engineer, carefully applied the brakes, looking ahead for any kind of obstruction, the conductor, on whose side the figure had been waving at them was looking hard at the trees.

"Bastard," he muttered. "Looks like some tourist backpacker thought it would be fun to give us a scare. As soon as you hit the whistle, he stopped waving and ran into the forest. Better go slow for a while, just in case, eh?"

The engineer just nodded. Being less sure that it was just a prank, she was intent on slowing the train while straining her eyes looking for any signs of trouble ahead.

The locomotive was soon deep into the forest so even had they looked back, neither the conductor nor the engineer would have seen the backpack-wearing figure jump onto one of the passing freight cars.

***

Nathan, for his part, had reacted instinctively to give chase to the Colonel. As a result, he hadn't given any thought to what he hoped to accomplish nor how to go about it.

Like the Colonel before him, he started to climb the mountain slope and hadn't gone far before a shot rang out and he actually heard the slug hit a nearby tree. That caused him to halt, and even freeze in place, before deciding to carry on. He had learned caution from this, however, so he moved as stealthily as he could. He too came across the spot where Oliver and Nathan had dug up the gold, and passed on. Sparing only a brief glance down to where Oliver (Jon), Hannah, and the two police constables were, he kept moving.

There was a slight trail, with the occasional footprint, leading up the mountain slope, which he followed. When it intersected the game trail, he didn't know whether to head east or west, but took a chance on right and was soon rewarded with more footprints. Further confirmation came when he reached the clearing at which the Colonel had stopped for his brief rest.

The rucksack was lying right there.

Although he didn't need a rest, he did stop to inspect the rucksack. Hefting it, experimentally, he then set it back down. Feels like about forty pounds, *he thought. Looking inside, he found four leather bags, each weighing about 10 pounds. The bags were full of gold coins!*

He must have had to lighten the load. So he dropped it! *Thought*

Nathan.

Encouraged, he shouldered the rucksack and continued his stealthy pursuit. When he came to the junction with the trail leading down-slope, he stopped to look around. There was the train tunnel, there the tracks, the stream, and the highway, and... THERE!... there was the Colonel! He was standing by the tracks near the edge of the forest... but what was he doing?

Being careful not to move, Nathan watched and listened. Then, he heard the echoing sound of the train in the tunnel. Looking back toward the forest, he saw the Colonel waving some kind of red flag over his head. Shortly after that he heard the train give a series of short blasts.

Nathan's eyes widened. You clever bastard! he thought, as he realized what the Colonel was going to do next.

Sure enough, as the train began to slow, and the three locomotives at its head disappeared into the trees, the Colonel popped out of the trees and ran up to the tracks watching for his chance to jump up on a passing car.

Nathan wasn't watching any longer though, he was running as fast as he could down the mountain trail.

He too was going to catch that train!

***

I had Silver search along each side of the tracks, all the way to the edge of the forest, but after each pass he just looked up at me as if to say: "*Gone.*"

Jack was standing beside the highway patrol car as Silver and I made our way up to join him.

"The train," I said. It was both a statement and a question.

Jack nodded. "A freight train. I saw the back end of it vanish into the forest before I could even get out of the car."

"Did you see anything else"

He shrugged. "Only the signal light shining back at me from the rear of the caboose," he said, ruefully. "How about you?"

"Silver followed the trail just fine. I didn't see either of them, or hear any more shots, but I heard three short toots from the train's horn.... The scent trail ended right beside the tracks, so I think one of them must have flagged the train down and hopped on."

"Both of them, you think?"

"I suppose so, otherwise Silver would have scented something."

"Hmmm. They would both have been on the other side of the train, so I wouldn't have seen them either way. What do you want to do?"

"That's the question, isn't it? Do we have a highway map?"

We did. Jack found one in the glove compartment of the police car. He spread it out on the hood of the car so we could look at it together."

"Looks like the tracks go to Kamloops," said Jack.

"Kamloops…"

"What are you thinking Alex?"

"I'm trying to put myself in the Colonel's shoes. I'm wondering what he would be thinking. If it were me, I think I'd try doubling back to see if I could convince Hannah to get away with me. But, in his case, I think he's too angry with her for that. I think he's more likely to try to make his escape, set himself up somewhere we can't find him, and maybe try to reconnect with Hannah sometime later."

"In that case," reasoned Jack, thoughtfully, "if it were me, I'd ride the freight all the way to Kamloops, then…"

"That's the question, isn't it?… Do you still have a train schedule with you? I left mine behind."

He did. Retrieving it from his carry-on bag, he spread it out on the hood of the car, on top of the map."

The next two VIA Rail 'on request' stops were Blue River and Clearwater, then a scheduled stop at Kamloops, the latter scheduled for 6:30 pm.

"It's nearly 2:30 now…" I started, then stopped.

"What?"

"He could just get off anywhere, but his style is strategy, remember? And he has time to think now that he's hiding on the train. What if he got off at Kamloops then re-boarded the VIA train?"

"If he still has his ticket, they'd have to let him back on," Jack reasoned. "And it's too soon to have rebooked his roomette, so he'd even get his room back."

"Yes, and if he rode all the way to Vancouver, he'd have a bigger city to hide out in. One with stores for coin collectors! If he only sold one coin at one store, he'd get over $200 for it. Sell another one at another store and he'd get another $200, all without raising any suspicions... and if the stores re-sold them to collectors, the Bank of Canada would never hear about it, and neither would we."

"Makes sense to me, but they'll never believe it," said Jack.

"Who?"

"Our bosses. They'll never believe it. They'll want to do ground searches everywhere that freight train stops or even slows down, and especially in every town or city along the way."

"My boss would believe it..." I reflected. "It's the way he thinks too – the way he'd do it himself. But I agree with you that others will see it differently. Tell you what. Let's radio it all in, tell them we're pursuing a lead in Kamloops, and ask them to pass it all along to Bob in Ottawa. That way, he'll know where we're headed and he or someone else can decide what else they want done."

"Is there time?"

"Let's see." We consulted the VIA Rail schedule again. "If it was on schedule, the VIA train would have passed through here around 11, but we were two hours behind at Jasper, so they probably passed through here about 1. The next two 'on request' stops are Blue River and Clearwater, then a scheduled stop at Kamloops at 6:30 pm. Let's call it 8:30 if they're still running two hours late.

"In that case, the freight train was about an hour behind them. The freight train gets priority over the passenger train so, somewhere up ahead, I bet the VIA train has to pull onto a side track and let the freight train pass it. If that takes half an hour, then the VIA train should get into Kamloops around 9 pm."

"And the Colonel could be there waiting for it!" finished Jack.

"Yes, and maybe with Nathan right behind him. I wish I knew what was going on in that boy's head!"

"You talked to him more than I did. What do you think?"

"I don't know. Could be that he wants to strike back at the Colonel for shooting his father, could be his way of trying to help Hannah. He seems so innocent sometimes. Maybe he's a bit of a Boy Scout trying to catch the bad guy."

"Let's hope not. He could catch a bullet," said Jack, darkly, then shook himself. "Let's see what we can do." Drawing his finger along the map he counted off the distances. "Looks like a little over 220 km to Clearwater, then another 125 km to Kamloops. The speed limit's 90 km/hr in the parks, then slower in the towns but higher on the highway outside the parks. Let's say four hours overall. We'll have to stop for gas along the way, but we can grab take-out food to eat as we go. Even with lights and siren all the way, we're probably still looking at four and a half hours."

I looked at my watch. "It's 4 o'clock now. If we're lucky, we can make the Kamloops railway station by, say 8:30 – it's going to be close!"

"Let's do it!" said Jack. "You've been doing all the work for the past hour, let me drive the first shift while you rest, and then we can switch when we stop for gas or food, OK?"

"OK!"

Once we were settled in, with Jack driving the highway patrol car, we hit the first snag in our plan. I couldn't reach a radio room in any detachment, ahead of us or behind us. I only had to look around to determine why. Unlike low frequency ham radios, which could bounce a signal off the ionosphere and practically 'skip ahead' great distances, our very-high-frequency, VHF, radios required line-of-sight. Deep down in valleys and surrounded on all side by towering mountains, we weren't going to be able to reach a detachment radio room until we got clear of the mountains.

"We're not going to be able to call this in until we get clear of these mountains, they're blocking the signal." I looked again at the highway map. There was no RCMP Detachment in Blue River, but there was one in Clearwater. We'd have to wait until we could get a signal through to them. Even so, it would take some time for them to relay the information to Jasper – which probably wouldn't be anything beyond informative – and to my boss Bob in Ottawa. It would be late evening in Ottawa by then. Even if it was decided to initiate a ground search, I doubted that anything would begin until the next morning.

"I think we're on our own again," I said to Jack, having summarized my thoughts.

Jack, as always, took it in stride. "Oh well, at least Jasper will know we didn't steal their highway patrol car," he joked. "You know, this is the fourth assignment I've been asked to help you out on, and I've been enjoying it. I'm still not cut out for the cloak-and-dagger stuff you always seem to get into, but they're exciting sometimes. I think they're growing on me."

"I'm glad Jack, because I'd have died several times over by now if you hadn't been around when I've gotten into trouble."

"All part of the job," he grinned, but I could tell he was pleased.

I had a lot more time to think, as we raced along the highway, but there were so many unknowns that I'm not sure that it did me any good.

Laurie Schramm

12 THE TIPPING POINT

Colonel James Peters (Ret'd.) had a lot of time to think as he sat at the end of an older-style grain car. His somewhat random choice had been a fortunate one as the inward sloping end-wall of the car created a small space at the end where he could sit, directly above the rearmost wheels.

He now regretted his stubborn insistence on taking the gold and running, especially since it had led to his arguing with and abandoning his daughter Hannah. Sixty years of obsessing on Jon's betrayal and being cheated out of his share of the robbery loot had just been too much to overcome, he thought. But, decades of military life had taught him that there was no point dwelling on what was past. You just had to pick yourself up and keep moving.

But moving where? *That was the question now.*

He had the gold. Fine. The police would be searching the Mount Robson area by now, probably with roadblocks along the highway, and they'd be organizing searches of the nearby towns. He should be able to hide out in Vancouver long enough to sell a few of the coins, spreading them out among several coin dealers, then he could buy an old car for cash and drive somewhere. If he drove south, he could look for a quiet place to cross the border into Washington State, giving him two more big cities in which to sell off more of the coins: Seattle and Spokane.

He had no worries for Hannah's safety. Fortunately, he hadn't told her of his real reasons for wanting to take the train trip and, although she now knew about some of his disreputable past, her standing up to him as she did would ensure that there were no legal repercussions for her to deal with.

Later, he could get a message to her so she'd know that he was safe... and to tell her that he was proud of her.

If only her mother could have seen the way she stood up to me, *he thought with fierce pride,* she'd have been proud too.

He'd have to watch out for the kid, Nathan, though. He hadn't had time to watch carefully, but if Nathan had been able to jump the train as well, then he would have to deal with that one last loose end...

***

The Reverend Nathan Risk was also thinking, as he sat at the end of another grain car closer to the end of the train. He was also reliving his previous hour's actions and questioning the wisdom of his impulsive decision to set off in pursuit of the Colonel.

Why had he done it? To get back at the Colonel for shooting his father? Some kind of vigilante-justice instinct? He wasn't sure.

It probably didn't even impress Hannah, *he thought.*

So, now what? Like the Colonel, he assumed that the police would be busy helping the injured and searching the highways and local towns.

They'd never guess he jumped the freight train, *he thought,* so maybe it's up to me now...

***

The freight train accelerated as it continued its journey south and it didn't even slow as it passed through Blue River. Continuing south and then turning west, it passed through Clearwater, again without stopping. It did slow down a bit, however, as it passed through Clearwater, and both the Colonel and Nathan were treated to the unbelievable sight of passing The Canadian *which stood on a separate set of tracks just outside of the town. Both of them immediately realized what that meant. This was the same VIA Rail train they had left in Alberta, the Colonel in Hinton, and Nathan and his father in Jasper. Clearly,* The Canadian *was running late and had been pulled over to let the higher-priority freight train pass it by.*

At this time, a well-placed observer, had there been one, would have seen the Colonel and Nathan do the exact same things: each pulled a timetable from his pocket and, consulting the schedule, realized that the next stop was Kamloops. Since the VIA Rail train was running late, it would be a quick stop — just enough to deal with embarking and disembarking passengers. That could be an advantage.

Who would ever expect me to get back on the original train? *thought the Colonel.*

Who would ever expect the Colonel to get back on the original train? *thought Nathan. Then he set his jaw firmly.* I guess I'll have to see this thing through...

***

The freight train finally slowed to a crawl as it entered the rail yards that precede the station on the north side of Kamloops. As it advanced, the Colonel looked around and, seeing no one around, jumped down from the grain car on which he had been riding. He checked his watch. It was 8:35 pm. So far, so good.

Hoping to look like a backpacking European tourist that had taken a wrong turn, he hitched his backpack up a little high on his back and walked purposefully towards the station. No one accosted him, he entered the station and made his way to the first available washroom to clean himself up as best he could. After that, he took a seat in the station's coffee shop and settled himself to wait.

It wasn't long.

***

The Colonel hadn't been accosted when he jumped off the freight train, but he had been seen. Nathan had been watching closely from his position close to the rear of the train, and had a clear view of the Colonel's exit. He also correctly interpreted the Colonel's attempt to look like a backpacking tourist and judged that he was unlikely to risk attracting suspicion by furtively looking around. Indeed, the Colonel adopted a very purposeful-looking stride in the direction of the station.

Nevertheless, Nathan took the precaution of jumping from his grain car to the opposite side of the track and walking along that side while the rest of the train continued past him, all the while blocking the view of anyone on the station side. When the caboose passed him by, its red rear signal light glowing in the evening twilight, he crossed the tracks.

Not wanting to risk confronting the Colonel in the station, where there might be a large number of innocent passengers and staff, he chose a bench in the station's parking lot from which he could wait for The Canadian *and also make sure that the Colonel didn't double-back and come out of the station.*

He didn't have long to wait, either.

***

At 8:50 pm, running two hours behind schedule, The Canadian *rolled into the station. Passengers wanting to stroll around the station were warned that the stop would be brief, so they should remain on the platform. Any passengers that chose to do so might have been mildly surprised to see that the front few cars had been disconnected from the train and were being pulled away to make room for an additional car, which was shunted in and then everything re-connected.*

As soon as the few disembarking passengers had left the platform area, the Colonel went up to board the train.

François was surprised to see him, but this was far from the first time that a passenger had disembarked from a train and then wanted to re-embark from a different station. He was a bit miffed not to have been informed in advance, of course, but then this has hardly the first time that had happened either. As a long-serving railway man, he had learned to take such things in stride and, as the Colonel's ticket was still valid and his roomette had not yet been re-assigned, he had no real reason for complaint. It was only after the Colonel had boarded that it occurred to him to wonder what had become of the Colonel's daughter, Hannah.

Whereas experience and instinct had enabled François to maintain a nonchalant professional demeanor in the face of the Colonel's surprise appearance, it took concentrated effort on his part to deal with the surprise, a few minutes later, of seeing Nathan show up seeking to board and re-establish himself in his former roomette. François was up to the challenge, however, and soon Nathan was on the train and heading for his sleeping car.

It belatedly occurred to him, that each of these latest two passengers had acquired a backpack somewhere along the way, and that neither of them seemed to have any of their former checked or carry-on baggage with them.

There's a connection there, he thought to himself, and it occurred to him to wonder whether these strange goings-on were connected to the two Mounties that had been on the train.

Shaking himself from these distracting thoughts, he checked his pocket watch, took a careful look along the train in each direction to ensure that all was in order, and called out "All Aboard!"

He was just about to pick up the small step stool that was always placed by the steps leading up to the train, when he sighted two more passengers – and a large dog that looked like a wolf – waving frantically to him from the far edge of the platform.

"Sacré bleu!"

***

Jack had turned off the siren a few blocks away from the train station, so as not to give any advance warning of our arrival. Pulling into a spot near the entrance we got out, grabbed our carry-on bags and ran through the station. We stopped on the platform side just in time to hear the "All Aboard" call. Not wanting to be easily seen, we stayed where we were and began waving at François, trying to attract his attention.

When he spotted us, his jaw dropped in surprise, but he was quick enough to stride over to us.

"François, did the Colonel get back on the train?" I asked.

"*Mai oui*, but just a moment ago, and the young reverend too!"

"OK, at least we haven't lost them. Are they in their same roomettes as before?"

"Yes, the same, why?"

"Because they're on the far side of the train. If they're hiding in their roomettes, they won't see us…"

"You wish to board, yes? The train leaves now."

"Yes, we do, but is there somewhere else we can stay? Somewhere they won't see us. We can explain later."

François thought for the briefest moment, then his eyes widened. He clearly had an idea. "*D'accord!*" was all he said. "Come with me."

François led us toward the front of the train, and up and into the car directly behind the baggage car that had been broken into. The door of this new car was locked and, when we went in, we found ourselves in a very unusual kind of car.

"We added a second baggage car, eh? so we have a locking door again. It was the easiest way – the car was just sitting here and we didn't have to move any of the baggage but it's secure again.

"You can see that this car is different. It's an older style that has a conductor's office and crew quarters. Since it's an extra car, the crew quarters are empty. There are berths and a communal washroom, but it's not fancy, eh? Not what you're used to."

It was a question.

"This will be great. Thank you!" I assured him.

He seemed pleased. "I can have food delivered here from the dining car. I'll bring you a menu…" Then, he seemed to remember his other responsibilities. "Will there be trouble?"

"I think so. There's been fighting, shooting even, and the Colonel is trying to escape, and he's armed. We would have asked you to stop the train while we wait for help, but he'd know if there was an unusual delay – especially after hearing you call the 'All Aboard' – and we don't want him to panic and try taking hostages."

As I was speaking, my words were underscored by the slight lurch of the train getting underway.

"Yes, I see," he said, seeming to notice for the first time the rifle that Jack had brought with him. "What do you want me to do?"

I looked at Jack for confirmation. When we were able to get radio reception, we had provided a summary of the situation to the radio room duty officer in the Kamloops Detachment and asked that it be relayed on to my boss in Ottawa. We hadn't stated any plans beyond following the Colonel and saying that we would advise further if and when we located him.

Jack just nodded.

I took a breath. "OK. What's the next stop?"

"Ashcroft, but only if someone requests it. That's four hours away"

"Four hours, so we have some time. What we'd like you to do is to come up with some excuse to quietly ask people to leave the sleeping car that has the Colonel's roomette. They can go anywhere else: the dining car, dome cars, coffee shop, anywhere but their sleeping car. Can you do that?"

He thought for a moment. "I can throw the breakers for that car. It will put them on low-power emergency lighting in the corridor, but the power will be off in the roomettes... I can tell them that we need to have someone check each room to find out where the short-circuit is... I'll offer them free drinks in the bar and the dining room while we're checking."

"That should work. Let us know when everyone's out, OK?"

"I will. It will take a while, though, and the emergency power is a battery system, so it only lasts so long, eh?"

There wasn't much for us to do but sit and wait while François set about his task. Silver was happy with the opportunity to get a bowl of water and a chance to rest. For my part, still feeling the effects of having spent over an hour tramping around the mountain when we were tracking the Colonel, I took the opportunity to get a shower and a clean shirt.

It took an hour, but François finally reappeared bearing news, a thermos of coffee, and a plate of sandwiches.

"Thought you might be hungry, eh?" he said, setting them down on a table in the vacant conductor's office.

"How did you make out with the passengers?" asked Jack.

"Not bad. I decided to move everyone forward, so I cleared out the Park Car too. Most people took it well enough and are in the dining room or the bar enjoying their free drinks. The reverend didn't want to go, but I finally persuaded him out. He insisted on taking his backpack with him, though, and he insisted in sitting in the Park Car. He's the only one there. I think he's watching to see if the Colonel emerges, eh?"

"And the Colonel?" I asked.

"A bit of a tense moment there..." he said, scratching his chin. "Heard me talking to the other passengers, eh? And stuck his head out the door to see what was up... I told him what I told everyone else, but in his case, I made it sound like more of a request than an order. I was sure he'd refuse.

"And he did refuse. He said he was staying put, wasn't interested in any damn-fool nonsense, didn't need any light, and didn't want to be disturbed. I put on my meek, conciliatory face, didn't argue with him, apologized for the disturbance, and left, eh?"

I breathed a sigh of relief. "Well done, François, that was quick thinking, and brilliant to think of clearing out the Park Car as well. But we've got to get Nathan out of there too. Would you please try one more time and try any excuse you can think of to get him up here with us?"

He agreed, and went off to try again.

A few minutes later, François was back with Nathan in tow.

"Hi Nathan," I said. "We need to talk."

I motioned for him to sit down with us.

"How did you know?" he asked.

"That you were here? We were tracking you and the Colonel. Silver lost the scent at the tracks on the far side of the train tunnel. We figured that both of you must have jumped the freight train. There are others looking for you elsewhere, by now, but we thought the Colonel might be brazen enough to get back on the original train, and it seemed like wherever he was, you might not be too far behind. We got on just as the train was pulling out of the station, and the conductor confirmed that both of you were on the train. So, here we all are." I paused for a moment.

"I assume you've been following him with some idea of getting even for shooting your father?"

"I guess so…" said Nathan, looking and sounding more confused than his usual innocent-appearing self. "At first, I just reacted, then I was angry. I had a lot of time to cool down on the freight train though. After that, it was mostly that I didn't want him to get away with it all. I was thinking that maybe I could slip off at the next station and call the police, you know?"

I looked at him. "Well, Constable McDonald and I are here now. Why don't you give me the gun, Nathan?"

He started. "You know about that?"

"I saw the cut-out in your bible."

"That was dad's idea. He's the one that gave me the bible. He was always worried about me, and how my work would put me into contact with all kinds of people. He insisted that I should have some way to defend myself if I got into a bad situation. Growing up in the States everyone has a gun, so I didn't think much about it before now."

"Well, handguns are restricted weapons in Canada. You shouldn't have brought it into the country, and you shouldn't have it with you now. At least you haven't shot or threatened anyone with it… or have you?"

"No," he said. "I'm not even sure that I could, you know."

"I know… why don't you give it to me, and let us deal with the Colonel? OK?"

Nathan hesitated for a moment, but I could see the decision in his eyes even before he grimaced, reached into a pocket and brought it out.

"Here. Careful, it's loaded."

It was an older-style Remington derringer, double barreled, and loaded in both barrels. "Thank you," I said, unloading it and placing the gun and both rounds into a pocket. "I have a very similar one that I carry myself sometimes."

I smiled.

"What's in the pack, Nathan?"

He surprised me by giving me one of his familiar, brilliant, wide-eyed, innocent looking smiles. "Gold!" he said. "It's full of gold coins. I found it on the trail. I figured that the Colonel dropped it so he could make better time, and I just kind of picked it up and brought it along… I guess you'd better take that too," he said, rather reluctantly. "It doesn't actually belong to me, you know."

I smiled again. "Well done, Nathan. You stay here and hang on to it for me for now, OK? I'm pretty sure there'll be a reward for this."

"What are you going to do?"

"I'm going to go talk to the Colonel. See if I can get him to come to his senses and give himself up. If that doesn't work, we'll keep him bottled up in his roomette until we get to Vancouver and we can get some help."

"But he's dangerous!"

"Thank you, Nathan… but so am I."

Most of the passengers had become used to seeing Jack, Silver, and I in uniform on the train, so I don't think we caused a stir as we made our way to the back of the train although the rifle Jack was carrying should have looked conspicuous to anyone paying attention. Mostly, people seemed to be chatting away quite animatedly. The normal social barriers to conversing with strangers had come down for those used to seeing each other day after day on the train, and the free drinks had probably helped lower them even further.

When we reached the last sleeper car, Jack stationed himself at the front, while Silver and I passed along, aiming for the Colonel's roomette. When I reached it, I turned to make sure Jack was watching and ready, which he was.

I raised a hand and pointed towards the Colonel's roomette. Jack nodded and patted the rifle he was holding. No one would be getting between him and the rest of the train and, thanks to François' quick thinking, there was no one near or behind us.

I didn't like having Silver with me, but I thought I might need him. I compromised by stationing Silver at the end of the sleeping car with instructions to 'guard.'

I decided, and hoped, that we'd isolated the Colonel about as well as we possibly could under the circumstances.

Now for the hard part, I thought.

Stepping up to the door of the Colonel's roomette, I took up a position well to the side – in case he became rattled enough to try shooting through the door – reached over and knocked.

"Go away!" was the response.

"Colonel, it's Constable Houston of the RCMP."

Silence.

"Remember me... Alex?"

Silence... then, "I remember you."

"Can we just talk for a moment. Please?"

"I'm not coming out, and you're not coming in... You know I'm armed right?"

"I know. No one's going to rush you, and you can stay where you are. I just want to talk, OK?"

"How did you find me?"

"You remember my partner, Silver? He's a tracking dog. We followed your trail around the mountain, then Silver lost the scent where the tracks came out at the other end of the tunnel. It seemed likely that you jumped the freight train that went through – that must have seemed like a gift from heaven to you. There was no way to tell what you'd do after that, but with all your experience in military strategy, it occurred to me that you might figure that no one would ever expect you to get back on the same VIA train you'd been on before. There'll be police looking everywhere else for you by now, but I decided to take a chance and see if you were here."

"And now here we are... Is Hannah OK?"

"She's fine. She went back to Jasper with two other Constables, Oliver Risk, and Ben Shaw. I think she's feeling pretty mixed-up and upset about you though."

"I've really messed things up this time. I'm not sorry I shot Jon, or Oliver as you know him, he had it – and worse – coming to him. That fool Ben should have had more sense too. I never wanted to hurt Hannah, though. She probably despises me now."

"I kind of doubt that, you know. I talked to her a bit on the train, and I think she has a pretty good head on her shoulders. She handled herself pretty well when all the violence broke out too. I can't pretend that she'll approve of some of the things you've done but, in my job, I have to study people pretty closely and I was paying attention to her reactions after the train had passed and you were gone..."

"And?"

"And she was focused on two things: helping us look after the two injured people and worrying about what was going to happen to you."

There was a long moan from inside the roomette.

"Colonel?"

"What?" The belligerence was gone now; replaced by despair.

"From what I know of your background you've done some bad things and also some good things in your life, some heroic things even. Maybe when Hannah looks back on it all the two will kind of cancel out. You know?"

Silence... then, another groan. At least he was hesitating.

"Look, you got your revenge on your former partner. You're not going to be able to keep the loot, but the others aren't going to get it either.... Why not call it a day before your legacy gets tarnished any further? You'll be able to talk to Hannah when things calm down... explain your side of the story."

"She'll never listen."

"Never is a very long time. Give the girl some credit. I know she still cares for you. I think she'll give you a chance."

More silence...

"Why not leave the guns behind and come out? Give her a chance, and a chance for a future."

"All right..." he said, after another long pause. "Give me a minute, will you?"

"Sure Colonel. Take your time... I'll be here when you're ready."

Looking back toward Jack, I raised a hand with my palm facing him, to let him know that we were at a critical juncture.

Seconds went by... then minutes...

"Colonel?... Are you OK in there? Do you need anything?"

Blam! The almost deafening blast of a .45 calibre gun going off in a confined space.

Damn! I thought. "Get François and a key!" I yelled to Jack, who turned and ran towards the front of the train, looking for the conductor.

But there's no rush now, I thought, looking at the still-closed roomette door as I leaned back against the outer wall of the corridor.

The Colonel would never be in a hurry again.

13 LOOSE ENDS

When François came and unlocked the roomette door for us, we found the Colonel half-lying with his back upright in one corner of the lower berth, beside the window. His .45 pistol had fallen to one side, and he looked peaceful, if you disregarded the layer of blood on both walls behind his head. When we went to check his pulse there was none, then his body crumpled forward revealing horror.

Part of the back of his head was partly gone, shot away as the slug he'd fired through the palate - the inner roof of his mouth - travelled up, through his brain, and then out again through the upper-rear of his skull.

I still get nightmares sometimes.

It could have been worse. We found all three guns. He could have tried to shoot his way out, and or take hostages.

Even after we evacuated the rail car, he could easily have shot me, then Silver, then who knows? Jack would have taken him down, of course, but Nathan could have been another casualty had he been brave – but foolish – enough to try to rush in.

But none of that happened because, in the end, although he was too stubborn to surrender, in his own way he tried to avoid more bloodshed for Hannah's sake. I know that, because he'd spent those last few minutes, when I was waiting for him to make his final decision, writing a last note. He was holding it in his other hand when we found him.

My Dear Hannah, it began.

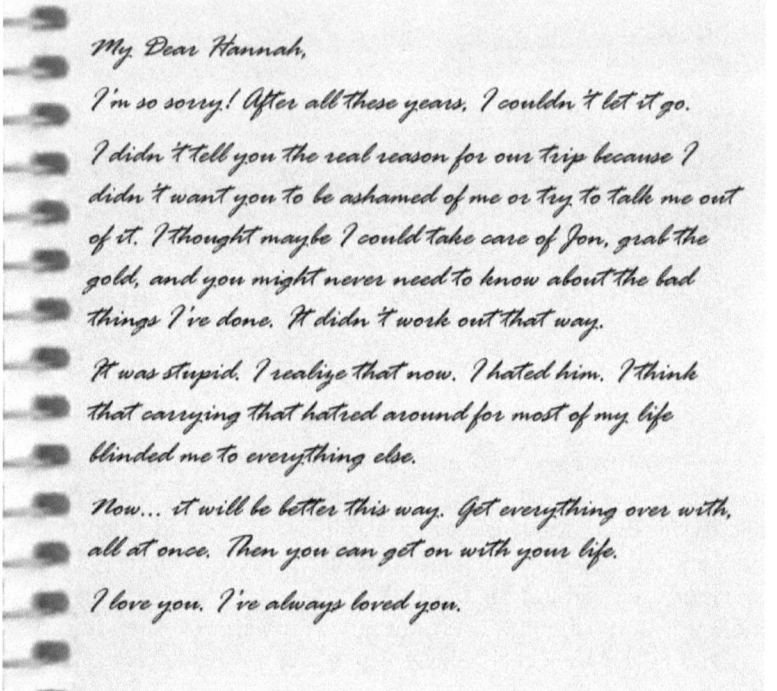

My Dear Hannah,

I'm so sorry! After all these years, I couldn't let it go.

I didn't tell you the real reason for our trip because I didn't want you to be ashamed of me or try to talk me out of it. I thought maybe I could take care of Jon, grab the gold, and you might never need to know about the bad things I've done. It didn't work out that way.

It was stupid. I realize that now. I hated him. I think that carrying that hatred around for most of my life blinded me to everything else.

Now... it will be better this way. Get everything over with, all at once. Then you can get on with your life.

I love you. I've always loved you.

With François' agreement, we moved the Colonel's shrouded body up to the mostly empty baggage car. We did the same with the confiscated guns and the two packs of the gold, so we could keep them secure. François then locked the Colonel's roomette from the outside, with his special key.

During all the action, the train had passed through Ashcroft, without stopping, and we were travelling through the Fraser Canyon towards Hell's Gate when François and Nathan found Jack and I collecting our thoughts and letting the adrenaline fade away, as we sat at a table in the crew quarters of the baggage car. The views from the train were spectacular, I suppose, particularly those from high up on the train bridge when we crossed the Fraser River, but we were no longer in the mood for it.

"Everything is settling down back there," said François. "Except for the young reverend here, so I thought I should bring him up here. OK?"

"Thank you, François, you're been great…. Hello Nathan, how are you feeling?"

"Oh, me? I'm OK. I guess I'm worrying about Hannah and my father…" He stopped abruptly, as he belatedly realized the order in which those words had come out.

"We understand. You know, you took some crazy risks, and really should have stayed put with your father and the others, but I'd like to say thank you. It was your scent that Silver was familiar with, and I think it was you that he was able to follow over to the mountain to the other side of the tunnel. If you hadn't followed the Colonel, we might never have been able to discover how he got away. If he'd made it to Vancouver, we might never have found him again either."

"We might never have found the gold you recovered either," added Jack. "Someone might have come across it years from now, or not. Even if it was later found, it might not have been by someone honest enough to turn it in."

"What will happen to me now?" asked Nathan.

"I think your future's pretty much up to you. Don't you?"

"You mean you're not going to arrest me?"

I glanced at Jack. "Well, you brought a restricted weapon into the country but you turned it in, you found some of the stolen gold and you turned that in, and you helped us catch a fleeing criminal that was armed and dangerous. I have to report it all to my boss, but I really don't think you have anything to worry about."

"That's a relief," he sighed. "I guess I'll have to try to find a way to get back to Jasper then."

"Yes, I think there are at least two people there that will be glad to see you."

"Will dad be arrested?"

"It's already happened. There was still a warrant out for his arrest from the original robbery. Whether the Crown Prosecutor decides to take it to trial though is another matter. Given your father's age, and the recovery of the gold, and everything else that's happened, I really don't know. I think that both your dad and Hannah are going to need your support right now though."

The train's next stop was at Boston Bar, and this time I asked François if I could use the radio phone in his office. Even though it was after midnight our time, so after 3 am Ottawa time, I dialed my boss' home number, woke him up, and gave him the whole story.

After that, there was nothing to do but try to get some sleep. We arrived in Vancouver on schedule, at 8 am, the next day.

Day 7
June 1, 1978

Colleagues from the Vancouver Sub-Division and the coroner's office met us at the station in Vancouver, and we signed over the backpacks full of gold and the confiscated handguns.

My boss had cleared us to go back to Jasper so we could type-up and file our reports related to Oliver Risk (Jon Hope) and Ben Shaw. Knowing that Nathan would be desperate to get to Jasper as well, we offered him a ride with us.

After a bit of work, we found a taxi driver with a van that was willing to take us from Vancouver to Kamloops, which took 4 hours. From there we retrieved the Highway Patrol Car we had left at the train station and drove ourselves the rest of the way to Jasper. It took five hours to drive nonstop to Jasper, as we had to obey the speed limit this time. It was pretty surreal driving through Red Pass, as we drove through Mount Robson Provincial Park, but otherwise a pleasant trip.

Ben Shaw had been treated and released from hospital, but was being held in the cells at the local detachment pending a court appearance the next day. Oliver Risk (Jon Hope) was still in hospital, undergoing observation to make sure his wounds had not been dangerously infected. Although it was late when we finally reached the hospital, they allowed us to see him in his room.

Nodding to the constable that was keeping an eye on Oliver's room, we let Nathan go in first. His cautious entry became jubilant, though, when he discovered that his father was awake and looking well, and that Hannah had been there keeping him company.

On the other hand, we had to tell Hannah what had happened to her father. Such duty is part of a police officer's life, and always a horrible duty to have to discharge. Fortunately, Nathan was there to help comfort her, so at least she wasn't alone with her grief.

Saying our goodbyes, we eventually left the three of them there and went to find motel rooms for the night.

"At least some good came out of all of this," I said, as we drove away.

"You mean Nathan and Hannah finding each other? You're a romantic, Alex," said Jack.

That sounded like the proverbial pot calling the kettle black, but all I said was: "Guilty as charged, Jack."

Days 8 and 9
June 2-3, 1978

We spent most of the next morning at the Jasper Detachment. Having returned the Highway Patrol Car, it took a while to type out our reports. I had brought the Colonel's handwritten note to Hannah with me and, although the original had to be kept as evidence for a while, I was able to make a photocopy to give to her.

The detachment had a vehicle that needed to be returned to their divisional headquarters in Edmonton, so they killed two birds with one stone by offering it to us so we could get there as well. After another visit to Hannah and the Risks, it took the rest of the day to reach Edmonton.

The next day, we flew out by commercial airline. We were on the same flight to Toronto, after which Jack changed to a plane for Halifax, while Silver and I took a flight to Ottawa.

14 EPILOGUE

Days 10 and 11
June 4-5, 1978

A few things happened fairly quickly after that. Between the shooting in Red Pass, the subsequent chase and capture in the Fraser Canyon area and, of course, the whole story of the stolen gold, we caused a brief media sensation. There was even a feature article being written for *Macleans* magazine.

We'd unintentionally upset the Officer in Charge (i/c) of the Kamloops Detachment, who handled the media questions well enough and managed to take most of the credit. But I could tell from the TV footage my boss had videotaped, that there was some simmering resentment that the case had been resolved by Jack, Silver, and I, rather than his own officers.

I was still part of the Security Service at the time, and based in Ottawa, while Jack was posted to a detachment in small-town Nova Scotia at the time. As a result, some members of the media were able to find Jack and I when we were briefly back in Jasper, and the Kamloops people weren't able to completely manage the news. That the Officer i/c took it a step further and complained about me within the Force, I was about to find out!

June 4 was a Sunday, but my boss, Staff Sergeant Robert (Bob) G. Simpson, wanted me to run through the whole adventure from start to finish with him, which we did at his house.

Bob seemed well satisfied, once I'd finished my story.

"They put up wanted posters with a very good sketch of him at the time. The trainmen had heard his partner call him 'Jon,' but no one knew his full name, where he'd come form, or where he'd gone."

Bob said that the Force had always suspected that he'd gone to hide out in the southern U.S., because that's where some of the stolen money had turned up, but neither the Force nor the FBI had been able to find the source of stolen bills. It was only because the FBI was investigating Oliver Risk for fraud, nearly sixty years later, that it was discovered that Oliver Risk was actually Jonathan Hope. It had taken all that time to finally track him down.

Slim Peters, later the Colonel, they'd quietly watched for all those years and Bob told me the 'untold' story of how they discovered when the Colonel had identified American Businessman Oliver Risk as the former Jon Hope. The original investigators in the Force had suspected the involvement of an 'inside man' with the gang, and even that it might be Ben's father, Robert Shaw, but the Colonel had refused to identify him and there was no hard evidence against him so nothing more could be done at the time.

When he discovered Oliver Risk's planned trip to Canada, Bob was immediately suspicious, and when he learned about the coincidence of the Risk's itinerary and that of the Peters, he was sure that 'the game was afoot' and decided to send me to keep an eye on them all, backed up by Jack.

"Kind of a long shot, though, after all those years. Don't you think?" I asked.

Bob smiled his 'Cheshire Cat' smile, that I'd gotten to know so well. "Nothing ventured, nothing gained, but I had a feeling..."

When Bob has 'a feeling,' criminals should cringe, I thought.

My world seemed to turn on its head the next morning, when Silver and I walked into the office, however.

"Come on!" said Bob as soon as he saw me, "The Assistant Commissioner wants us in his office ASAP."

Uh-oh, I thought.

"What's up?" I asked, hastening to keep up as he strode down the hallway to Assistant Commissioner George MacLeod's office.

"I think we're about to find out," he said, as we were waved directly into the Assistant Commissioner's office.

It had been Assistant Commissioner George MacLeod that had talked me into leaving the Metropolitan Toronto Police Force for the RCMP four years earlier, and when I had graduated from training, he had been the one to make sure I was assigned to remote, small-town policing at first. When Silver had come into my life, he had been the one to see the potential for the first woman graduate and a dog, that looked nothing like a conventional police dog, to work undercover. When he had assumed command of the RCMP Security Service, he had asked me to transfer there as well, which is how I'd come to work for Bob for previous three years. In all that time, I'd developed an immense respect for the Assistant Commissioner but, in all honesty, I was still a bit afraid of him too.

Perhaps part of it was the 'parade-ground' voice that he seemed to be able to switch on or off at will, and which – at full volume – rivaled even that of the Depot Division Sergeant-Major from my training days.

He used it now.

"HOUSTON!"

At times like this, one doesn't get asked to take a chair and relax. One comes to rigid attention a few paces from the front of the desk, calls out "Yes, Sir!" and waits for the axe to fall. I tried not to flinch physically, but I sure did mentally.

"I have a telex here from the Officer i/c Kamloops Detachment, demanding your head."

Uh-oh, now I thought I knew what was coming.

Waving the telex form in the air, the Assistant Commissioner continued: "He says that, with a known criminal and gunman on the train you jumped on yourself and played some kind of damn-fool game to apprehend him that put countless passengers and crew at risk, when what you should have done is stopped the train and waited for the ERT[19] to arrive and deal with it."

He paused and looked at me, but it was a rhetorical pause, and I knew better than to say anything, yet.

"Now then," he said, ratcheting the volume down just a little. "What have you got to say for yourself? No, Staff-Sergeant, don't bother trying to jump to her defense - I want to hear it first-hand."

"Well Sir, he's correct, as far as it goes… but it would have taken at least two hours to call-up the nearest ERT team and get them all the way from Kelowna to Kamloops. Long before that, the Colonel would have realized that he'd been found and he was too good a military strategist to have just sat there waiting while we had reinforcements on the way. I was afraid that he would judge that his best bet was to brazen it out, take hostages even, and bulldoze his way out, even if it meant ultimately going down in a blaze of glory. As a military veteran of two wars, and well-armed as he was, he had the experience for it. I was also afraid that he'd have had time to realize that he'd already made a few mistakes and that desperation might be clouding his judgement.

"On the other hand, I judged that if we could let the train proceed and evacuate the entire train car, that I might be able to talk him down - get him to think about the legacy he'd be leaving his daughter – and that maybe he'd come around to being sensible and surrendering. At that point, I was only risking my own life – and that of Silver's."

It was only then that I realized that, instead of lying by my side, which would have been normal protocol, Silver had been sitting on his haunches, looking directly at the Assistant Commissioner, and listening. He was acting as if he were on trial too!

The Assistant Commissioner just sat there for a moment, looking at me without speaking, but I avoided flinching again, held his gaze, and shut up. I'd said my piece. Finally, he shifted in his chair and shifted into a very quiet tone.

"So, you didn't know about the dynamite then?"
"No Sir."
"But you suspected it, didn't you?"
I shifted my shoulders just a little bit and tried to put some life into my voice. "Yes, I suspected it... he'd worked with explosives his whole life. I thought it might have seemed natural for him to have brought along a stick or two of dynamite. That's partly why I didn't try to send Silver away. He's trained to detect explosives, and I hoped that if the Colonel had dynamite with him and reached for it, that Silver might give me an extra second or two of warning."

"And you would have too, wouldn't you?" said the Commissioner, looking directly at Silver for the first time.

"*Grruph!*" answered Silver. He might not know all the words, but Silver had an uncanny ability to follow the rough sense of my conversations, as the Assistant Commissioner well knew.

He smiled then, the Assistant Commissioner, and his penetrating gaze came back to me as he rose from his chair, tore the telex form in half and dropped it into his wastepaper basket. "That will about do for the Officer i/c's complaints," he said.

"Sir?"

"Look. Bob filled me in, and I've already had a chat with a few other people. You were on the spot. You knew the circumstances and the psychology. You assessed the risks. You came up with a plan, and you, your colleagues, and the VIA Rail conductor, carried it off. Too bad the Colonel decided to end it all, but no one else got hurt. Perhaps it's all for the best. I don't really give a damn about the recovered gold, but let's call that icing on the cake. The important thing is that... You. Did Well!" and he actually, very seriously, saluted me!

Before I could think of anything to say, he went on.

"Do you remember our first meeting back in 1974, when my friend, your Captain, on the Metro Toronto force recommended you, and I asked you to join us instead?"

"Yes, Sir."

"Well, I have to go to Toronto now and meet with him in person for two reasons. One: to tell him that he did us a big favour, because you're the best thing that has happened to the Force in many years – and if either of you ever tells anyone what I just said I'll have your spurs[20]. Understand?"

"Yes Sir," Bob and I both said, in perfect unison.

"The second reason I'm going to Toronto – and I want you to come with me - is because I want to see the look in your old Captain's eyes when he sees your Corporal's stripes."

At that he reached over to his desk and picked up a shiny new pair of gold laced corporal's stripes, the formal kind that go on a red serge, and held them out. "Bob, I think you should be the one to present these."

"Yes, Sir!" said Bob for the second time.

As he did so, my mind started functioning again. "But Jack was part of it all too, and I only have four years' service," I said.

"Yes, Constable McDonald did a good job on this assignment. He'll get a Commissioner's Commendation for it. As for the years' service, it's the quality of the service not the time, and we gave you credit for your time on the Metro Toronto police force. There's lots of precedent for that. But, at the end of the day, it was up to the Commissioner. It was actually his idea, although I completely agree with him, and I'm certainly not going to tell you that the Commissioner said "Promote her! And for God's sake keep her away from office jobs. Put her back out in the field where she belongs!"

Jack did get his commendation, and was both surprised and well pleased with it.

Bob and I, together, wrote an official letter to VIA Rail Canada, commending François for his assistance through the railway parts of the case, and I heard from him later that he received a nice pat on the back from the company in consequence.

A few days later, Silver and I drove to Toronto for the Colonel's funeral. We were mostly there to support Hannah. Funerals are for the living, I've always felt. But we also wanted to pay our respects to the part of the Colonel that had been a highly decorated military veteran whose service had included two overseas wars.

It was a grey day, and I had time to reflect, as we stood there in the rain, me in my seldom-worn red serge, and Silver wearing his RCMP mini-shabrack[21] dog jacket with its yellow stripe around the border and the famous yellow 'MP' brand in the lower back corner on each side. He'd been awarded that for 'outstanding service while on duty' several years earlier[6].

I don't know how the balance of the Colonel's life should be added up, but he put his life on the line for our country many times over, and that seemed to outweigh the other things he'd done as I looked at his coffin, draped with the Canadian flag, with his many medals resting on top.

Sometime later, the Bank of Canada confirmed that – amazingly – every single gold coin was accounted for. All 1,200 of them, comprising 400 $10 coins and 800 $5 coins. Needless to say, the bank was happy to get the gold back, although they had long since written it off. They did pay Nathan a reward for his role in recovering some of the horde, and they even presented him with one of the original $10 coins as a souvenir. A very nice touch, I think.

Sometime after that, Silver and I attended another ceremony. We'd been invited to Nathan and Hannah's wedding. The last I heard he'd received his congregation assignment and they were living in an outport community on the Labrador coast. The Newfoundlanders and Labradorians would be amused by his wide-eyed innocence, and they would love his infectious smile, I thought.

I do love a happy ending.

Laurie Schramm

… Corporal Houston and Silver will return,
in *An Intrepid Mountie.*

Laurie Schramm

SUMMARY

RCMP Constable Alexandra Houston sets out on a cross-Canada train journey to look for security vulnerabilities in advance of an upcoming VIP trip. At least, that's her cover assignment. In reality, Alex, Silver – her police-service-dog partner – and colleague Const. Jack McDonald, are after bigger game. Against a backdrop of beautiful, constantly-changing countryside, Alex notices some strange behaviours on the part of several of her fellow passengers. As her journey continues from Canada's Atlantic Provinces, through Central Canada, and then westward across the Prairies, the behaviours resolve into break-ins, intrigue, and a growing certainty that quite a few people on the train besides herself are not who they seem to be.

Laurie Schramm

ABOUT THE AUTHOR

Laurie Schramm comes from an RCMP family, grew up while living in the RCMP Barracks (Depot Division) in Regina, Saskatchewan, and spent several summers working as a civilian for the RCMP while in high school and university. Early personal influences included not only the real-life RCMP culture but also Hollywood's versions via such classics as Rose Marie, and Susannah of the Mounties. Many of the events described in this novel are based on the author's real life, although not necessarily within an RCMP context.

For more information, see Laurier L. Schramm on **Linked in**

and:

www.laurieschramm.ca

or

www.facebook.com/LaurieSchrammBooks

Laurie Schramm

ENDNOTES

1. This part of the story was inspired by a real-life train robbery on August 2, 1920, in which CPR train No. 63 was stopped in the Rocky Mountains and robbed by three men. *See* Robert Collins, "Canada's Last Great Train Robbery," *Maclean's Magazine*, 15 February 1958, https://archive.macleans.ca/article/1958/2/15/canadas-last-great-train-robbery.

2. Colt 'Model 1902' double-action revolvers were produced in 1902 for the U.S. Army. They were actually Model 1878 revolvers fitted with 6-inch barrels and chambered to fire .45 calibre rounds. The 'double-action' feature meant that the trigger was used to both cock and discharge the revolver.

3. The source for this quote is: Richard Saunders, *Poor Richard's Almanack*, 1735, published by Benjamin Franklin, Philadelphia. The almanac was actually written by Benjamin Franklin and was published for many years under the pseudonyms 'Poor Richard' and/or 'Richard Saunders.'

4. On December 6, 1917 two cargo ships collided in the Narrows, which connected the Bedford Basin with the rest of the Halifax Harbour. One of the ships, the *SS Mont-Blanc*, was carrying high explosives. When a fire that broke out on the *Mont-Blanc*

reached the high explosives there was a massive explosion that destroyed most of Halifax's North End, killing some 2,000 people and injuring approximately 9,000 more.

5. See *An Inconvenient Mountie* (ISBN: 978-1-9994940-0-1).

6. See *An Inconspicuous Mountie* (ISBN: 978-1-9994940-2-5).

7. See *An Indestructible Mountie* (ISBN: 978-1-9994940-4-9).

8. See *An Inseparable Mountie* (ISBN: 978-1-7772424-0-4).

9. At this point in time, it was still part of the RCMP Years later, in 1984, the Security Service was spun-out to create the present-day Canadian Security Intelligence Service (C.S.I.S.).

10. See *An International Mountie* (ISBN: 978-1-9994940-6-3).

11. See *An Indispensable Mountie* (ISBN: 978-1-7772424-2-8).

12. French for "don't worry about it," or "it's not worth fussing about," a shortened version of *"Il n'y a pas de quoi."*

13. See *An Inseparable Mountie* (ISBN: 978-1-7772424-0-4).

14. The Canadian National Railways Police (CN Police) carry out dedicated policing focused on CN infrastructure. Its members are granted the powers of police constables under Canada's *Railway Safety Act*.

15. "At Scene."

16. "Message Received."

17. "Temporarily Out of Service."

18. "Location."

19. The RCMP first established Emergency Response Teams (ERTs) in 1977, beginning with ERTs based in 31 locations across the country.

20. Meaning "I'll have you fired."

21. Dating back to at least the 18th century, the shabrack (or shabraque) was originally a large cloth placed over, or under, the saddles of European cavalry. At some point it became traditional to add a border of contrasting colour, and to display a crest or other symbol in the lower-rear corner. The RCMP shabrack, which is placed under the saddle, seems to have originated in 1887, at about the same time as "MP" was registered as the horse

brand of the North West Mounted Police. It is black with yellow trim and displays the MP brand, topped by the Royal Crown, displayed (also in yellow) in the lower-rear corner on each side.

Laurie Schramm

ADVENTURES OF THE FIRST WOMAN MOUNTIE

Book 1: *An Inconvenient Mountie*
Book 2: *An Inconspicuous Mountie*
Book 3: *An Indestructible Mountie*
Book 4: *An International Mountie*
Book 5: *An Inseparable Mountie*
Book 6: *An Indispensable Mountie*
Book 7: *An Inexorable Mountie*
Book 8: *An Intrepid Mountie*
Book 9: *An Intimate Mountie*

www.laurieschramm.ca

Laurie Schramm

Adventures of the First
Woman Mountie

Laurie Schramm